SIMON SAYS

An Extreme Horror Novel

Ash Ericmore

SIMON SAYS

CHAPTER 1

Simon really hated his job. He *really* hated it. He worked in an office block where some smart arse had rented one side of the building out as random office space, and the other side of the building was to the local unemployment office. Four storeys of it. He didn't even know what the companies on the left side of the building did, per se. Sure, he knew what the companies were called—it's not like he couldn't read, he wasn't thick—but he had no direct dealing with them.

Except what he saw when they left stuff lying on their desks. And sometimes what they left in their drawers. But that was a whole different story.

The tossers on the right hand side of the building all worked for the social security. Pen pushing pricks that thought they were better than everyone else. There was a public entrance, but that was on the other side of the building, and none of the salt of the earth unemployed lads came into the building, proper. Just the office workers. Those on both sides.

In the centre of the building was the stairwell and lift, and on each floor was a couple of toilets. Communal between the companies, one for the blokes, and one for the birds. That's where Simon was now. He was looking down into a bowl full of human shit and piss.

One of the cunts hadn't flushed it.

It made the whole fucking bathroom stink. Bloke's bathroom, of course. The women's shitter had its problems, but this happened far more often over on this side, the dirty bastards. What made it worse was that it had obviously happened earlier in the day. A little experience told you that, by the way the shit congealed around the porcelain. And no fuckbag had flushed it all day. Tossers in ties pushing the door of the cubicle open and seeing it, curling their fat fucking faces up and screwing up their nose before moving on to the next cubicle.

Simon shivered as the hate flowed through him.

The anger.

Everything would be so much easier if people were just a little bit *decent*.

DON'T CLEAN IT.

Simon sighed, the rotten stink getting up his nose. "I've got to."

NO YOU DON'T. DON'T CLEAN IT. FUCKERS.

Simon raised his foot up and poked at the flush of the toilet with his trainer. He didn't want to get any closer to the bowl than he already had. Not until at least some of it had disappeared around the u-bend. He caught the handle with his sole and the toilet gushed a few litres of clean water out onto the shit. The bowl started to fill as the water landed on top of the island of shit and didn't push it down and away, and there was that brief moment of wonder: is the shit going to give and the toilet flush, or is the shit going to hold and the water going to overflow? It was fifty-fifty for a few seconds and then the island of shit plowed to the depths like Atlantis and the water level dropped. Simon breathed out a sigh of relief.

YOU ARE SUCH A JOB'S WORTH.

That was probably true. He waited for the foam to die down and then he looked over the rim to the water line. Bleach. It needed bleach. It probably needed a lot more than that, but he was pushed for time this evening, and he wanted to get out when he was supposed to. Simon turned to the trolley parked behind him and pulled out the ten-litre container of toilet cleaner. He popped the top off and glugged a couple of mugs worth down onto the water. That would have to do. Then he moved onto the next cubicle.

This one didn't have toilet paper, but at least it wasn't full of shit.

Simon burst out of the front of the building. King's House, it was called. It was about as royal as a polyp growing off his arsehole, though. He looked at the time. Six-thirty. He ran across the bridge to the road—it sounded fancier than it was, with the car park moating the building at basement level—and he jogged over to the bus stop. He'd stopped driving a couple of years back when it became cheaper to take the bus, even getting rid of his motor altogether. There was an old bloke standing at the stop, already waiting. As soon as Simon stopped the old man gave him a look. The sort of look you give someone when they're lying unconscious in the curb with donor kebab vomit around their chin at one in the morning. Simon would have wondered why, but there was nowhere for him to shower before he got home. He thought about buying a t-shirt that said *I smell of shit because of my job*, but thought better of it. He just looked at the ground uncomfortably.

FUCK HIM UP.

"No," Simon replied.

The old man looked at him, this time like he was a mental patient.

Also, not a surprise. Other people couldn't hear the devil on Simon's shoulder. He'd turned up about three weeks ago. In the cartoons there was always a devil and an angel, but Simon had lucked out and only got the devil. He couldn't see him, but imagined that he looked like a devil. He knew he was there, though, and that he wasn't a mental case as he himself had first suspected. He could see him out of the corner of his eye, just there in his peripheral vision, but when he looked—actually looked—he was gone. Invisible. After a day or two of ignoring this ranting little bastard, Simon had given up on pretending he wasn't there, and had started interacting with it. Only a little at first. *How are you, who are you, what the fuck, am I crazy?* That sort of thing. He'd found the little shit demon to be quite the gent, once you got by the swearing and death threats. Weirdly, the miniature hell-spawn had said that its name was also Simon. So as not to cause confusion in Simon's own head, he had deemed the hellion rug rat, Little Simon.

Little Simon had assured Simon that he was in fact just an embodiment of his own self-doubt, as caused by the girl that rejected him at the club the night before he had appeared, and that he was only there to help. It sort of made sense. True, Simon had been worse for wear that night, but he did remember hitting on some chick in the bar. Vaguely, he recalled, she was a three. Maybe a four. She'd said something about rather seeing the prick of a cactus, and walked away from him. It was a bit hazy because of the drink, and very loud in there. But it *felt* like that was what had happened.

Then there had been a kebab. Perhaps a small kip in the gutter.

Either way, the next morning, lo and behold: Little Simon.

Now, after three weeks of Little Simon ranting—sometimes psychotically—into Simon's ear, and absolutely guaranteeing that he was only verbalising Simon's own deep dark little desires, Simon had started to take slightly more note of him.

Little Simon was perhaps his own unfiltered thoughts.

And that thought gave Simon a little freedom. His own self telling him what he really wanted. Someone cheering his corner to really get Simon to score some goals.

Simon was beginning to really feel that Little Simon had his back.

PUSH THE CUNT IN FRONT OF THE BUS.

"No," Simon hissed as the bus slowed by the stop. The old man looked at him again and when the doors weeped open, got on, flashed his bus pass, and hobbled down the bus hurriedly, probably trying to escape Simon, or at least, his smell. Simon followed him on, and flashed his weekly pass at the driver.

"All right, Si." It wasn't a question, more a greeting, and came from the driver that Simon saw nearly every night.

Simon nodded at him and took the steps up to the top floor of the bus. He didn't want to see the old man anymore. The way he looked at him, it made him feel like he'd done something wrong.

YOU CAN FUCK HIM UP. HE DESERVES IT.

Simon looked around the top deck. Empty. Good. He went and sat at the front. There was something special about sitting at the front of a bus, looking out over the people below. There always had been, but he so rarely got the luxury. When he was at school he had to take the bus on occasion and the little bastards that rode it back then treated him like shit. He didn't even try for the top deck in those days. That's where the *cool* kids sat. But not now. Now he sat there. Maybe that made *him* a cool kid.

He watched as the street lights started to come on as the bus rounded the streets towards the harbour.

No it didn't. It made him a sad pathetic loser, rocketing towards middle age, and the cleaner of a shitty office block, with shitty workers. It made him envious. Angry. It made him think about the past and think about the mistakes he'd made. It made him regret being … him.

Little Simon's shoulders slumped. Simon saw it in from the corner of his eye.

THERE'S NO NEED TO BE LIKE THAT. COME ON. IT'S FRIDAY. WE CAN GO OUT. THAT ALWAYS MAKES US FEEL BETTER.

CHAPTER 3

Simon pulled a shirt on over his head while flipping his thumb against his phone looking for Jacko's number. He checked his teeth in the mirror and thumbed the number. It rang once.

"Boyo," Jacko answered. "'Ow doin'?"

"Fifth?"

"Nah, mate. Me chompers pan'd up una whizzin' on ..." he paused for a second and Simon could hear the rattle of a pill bottle. "... Tramadol."

Simon could barely understand the northern git at the best of times but he'd run out of other people to invite to the club. "So ... no?"

"Nah. Next week, ya?"

The phone went dead, and Simon just stared at it.

I DON'T KNOW WHAT YOU NEED OTHER PEOPLE FOR WHEN YOU'VE GOT ME.

Simon shook his head. "No, but no one else can see you and that doesn't make you much of a wingman." He looked at himself in the mirror one last time, with the thought of not going at all hanging there in front of him.

QUICKLY CLEAN UP THE BEDROOM. I GUARANTEE YOU'LL SCORE TONIGHT.

Simon looked himself in the eyes, the shape of Little Simon vaguely there, on his shoulder, disappearing as he looked directly at him to say,

"You'd better be right, or this is the last time."

The music in Fifth Avenue Night Club thumped. It made Simon unsure that he wanted to be there, and that, coupled with his lack of companionship had compiled his doubts. Even coming in, the bouncers on the door had given him *that look*. He knew what *that look* meant. It meant, *What's this ugly sack of skin doing coming down here on his own, like he's going to score*, and then they'd all laugh at him. At least, that's what it meant in his head.

He was standing at the bar looking around as casually as someone alone at a night club could look, all the while Little Simon was humming along to the music. How he could even hear the rhythm, he didn't know, let along be enjoying it. Weirdly—or not, as Simon was coming to understand—he could hear Little Simon over the music without issue, again raising the question as to Little Simon's actual physical presence.

WHAT ABOUT THAT ONE?

Simon looked around. He'd had a couple of beers already and he was feeling a little light headed. He'd also found that when he drank alcohol it seemed to effect Little Simon too, but quicker. The little demon seed got shit faced on a half of shandy. Simon's eye's fell on a woman in tight dress. She was younger than Simon. Skinny. Attractive. An eight, at least. Within a sudden break in the music, he said, "Fuck off," too loudly. "I'd never bang that."

Of course, that *wasn't* exactly what he'd meant. What he *had* meant was that he and the woman would never hook up biblically, simply because she exceeded his perceived league, when it really sounded to everyone around him that he *wouldn't touch that munter with a barge pole.*

In the split second of silence, you could see the look on the woman's face morph from shock to surprise, and finally to apoplectic. She looked at Simon—who quickly looked away—and then down at herself. There was the briefest of times when you could see her weighing up what she had seen. Him. Her. She assessed whether there was something wrong with her, something that perhaps she hadn't seen when she left for the club, or something that had happened since she had arrived. She checked to make sure there was no toilet paper stuck to her shoe, or that her dress hadn't unzipped itself.

She looked at Simon like he smelt of shit—which he didn't.

Now, as she had decided that there was nothing wrong with her, she looked at Simon and quickly judged him. It wasn't hard. At this point he had turned bright red and was hoping upon hope that spontaneous combustion was a thing and while odds were against it, it *could* happen right now. She strode over to him and he could see that she was thinking about tossing the drink she had in his face.

YOU FUCKED THAT UP.

"If you want to throw that in my face," he stammered. "I understand completely and would happily buy you another."

She scrunched her face up, but her demeanour didn't change.

"I'll buy you another if you want to throw that over me," he repeated, almost shouting to be heard over the music.

The cogs in her face changed, and then she proceeded to throw her drink into Simon's face. The laughter of the people around them was clear over the volume of the music. Then she waved the glass in his face, reminding him of his promise and she took him by his tie and led him away.

Simon followed like a puppy on a lead as this woman pulled him through the club and to the stairs, up to the next floor, where the music was muted and there was a balcony overlooking the sea. Simon, although not entirely opposed to being dragged through the club like this, avoided the stares of the other clubbers. The woman was far more attractive than he, and this was a good thing. This weird BDSM—if you will—play thing that was happening could only be good for his image, and when it was done, perhaps he might come out of this unscathed.

At the top of the stairs, she pulled him over to the bar and released him. "Vodka tonic," she said. "Large." She sounded local. She had that south of England twang that everyone from up north thought was posh, when in truth, it was only one dropped 't' from being something out of Eastenders.

Simon rifled through his pocket and pulled his wallet out, resting it on the bar and waiting for the chap in the waistcoat to come over. He glanced at the woman, trying not to look like he was looking at her. She was pretty. She had dark hair, below the shoulder and this tube dress that she looked like she had been poured into. Simon tried to work out how it worked while the two of them waited in silence. It looked like she had to lie on the floor and wiggle into it. He noticed that she was looking at him, and that he was staring at her body. *Shit.*

"Got an eyeful?" she said. She was half smiling, like she enjoyed the attention, but didn't want to admit it.

FUCK HER.

Simon ignored him and looked away from her, back down the bar. She tugged on his sleeve pulling his attention back. Now she was smiling. "No need to be like that," she said. "I'm Brett," she said.

Brett? That's a man's name?

TOO FUCKING RIGHT.

"Simon," he said, thrusting his hand out like he was at a job interview.

She looked at it and smiled. Her face implied she thought he was being cute, which was just as well, because being charming had disappeared off the table now that he was … sticky with her last drink. The barman came over and Simon ordered her a new drink and a bottle of beer for himself. He didn't specify what sort and the guy didn't ask. It was one of those places.

"You here alone?" she asked.

Simon nodded, sliding her drink down the bar to her.

"You don't say much." She took her drink and sipped it, looking around.

SHE'S GETTING BORED. SAY SOMETHING.

"So how about you? You here with friends, or can I keep you company?" It was a shit line, sure, and the huff that came from Little Simon spoke volumes about how much he agreed, but it seemed to restore her attention to him.

"I usually come down here on my own. My friends are all squares," she said. She seemed sad about it.

"Come on, then. Let's be alone together." Simon pointed at one of the few empty tables lining the room. She looked, nodded, and started over to them. The barman returned with Simon's change. Simon nodded smugly at him. *That's right,* he thought, *I, Simon the Unattractive, ruler of Birchingate, Scrubber of Toilets, am to sit with an eight.*

CHAPTER 4

Brett—whose real name was Brittany, Simon had discovered—was pretty solidly sloshed by eleven. Simon wasn't intentionally trying to get her drunk but without any of the usual boys present, he had found himself drinking too much, and accidently plying her with more than she was used to. Little Simon had apparently blacked out and regained consciousness at least twice in the last couple of hours, judging by his intermittent bouts of silence, and one rather off-putting session of snoring.

Simon helped Brett from the club, his arm around her waist, while she had hers slopped over his shoulder. He even saw an appreciative nod from the bouncers. Nice.

EVEN I'VE GOT A HARD-ON.

The drunk little pervert was getting on Simon's wick, but he supposed the little shit was right. It wasn't the only thing he was hoping was going to get on his wick. He giggled internally at his own dry, yet sharp, wit. Little Simon started hiccupping. That was all he needed. He veered Brett towards the taxi rank over by the curb. It was still early enough that more people were arriving than leaving and getting into a cab was easy. He helped Brett into the back and then followed her in. She started pawing at his face, and it crossed his mind that she'd had too much to drink and he didn't want to take advantage.

"Where to?"

Simon waited for a second, thinking. An internal struggle, between *my place* and wherever the hell it was that she lived. "Yours," she said, putting her fingers in Simon's mouth.

After he pulled his head away from her, he told the cabbie his address and they were off.

Surprised he'd gotten this far, Simon fished in his pockets for his house keys. He lived on the shitty estate at the edge of town—once a council estate, now full of run down properties with drug dealer tenants owned by slum lords who lived in the smoke. He lived on an okay street, he supposed. There was little noise at night, and most people didn't have either a sofa or a fridge in the front garden. He was trying to hold Brett up at the same time.

"Let me do that," she said. She pushed her hands into his jeans pockets and started fannying around with his cock. She was making it hard, which seemed to please her, but it was uncomfortable in his jeans, and they were still technically in the street. He giggled feigning great enjoyment and pulled away from her, releasing her hands. "Ah," she said with great glee. "You like to pull out, huh?"

Simon stopped for a moment trying to put two and two together, and then realised it was a sex thing. "Oh, yes." He smiled at her hoping that was the right answer and then fumbled his keys out and opened the front door. "In you go." She stumbled over the threshold and he followed her closing the door. "Would you like a coffee?"

She looked at him like he had just dropped out of the anus of extra-terrestrial. "No, I don't want a fucking coffee," she said. "I want … a fucking."

This evening had gone better than expected, Simon felt as she crashed into him, nearly knocking him from his feet. *Much better*, in fact. She was working his belt and trying to get his jeans down. He took her hands and stopped her, kissing her sloppily. Then he turned and hurried up the stairs keeping her hand in his. They reached the top of the stairs and she started working on his jeans again, trying to get them down.

He decided that this wasn't just going well or better, but going great.

She finally managed to get his jeans unbuttoned and pulled them down to his calves.

WAHAY.

Little Simon was awake. At least the hiccups were gone. *Shut up*, he thought to himself, hoping Little Simon would get the picture. There was no way he was going to perform with a commentary from that little shit.

"Look at the size of it," she said, sliding down and pulling his pants around his ankles.

Should have worn boxers instead of y-fronts. She took his cock in her mouth and started bobbing back and forth. Simon could see Little Simon stroking himself from the corner of his eye. "Must you?" he muttered.

Brett stopped. "Huh?" She looked up at him.

"Nothing," Simon added, and put his hand on her head, guiding her back to him.

She giggled and stood back up. "Bedroom?"

Simon could just about muster the brain power to point to the door on the left of the landing. His house was small. Pitifully small, to be honest, and the first floor held nothing more than one bedroom and a bathroom. Most of the other houses in the street had some conversion done with two bedrooms made on the first floor and the bathroom placed in an extension downstairs, but that wouldn't have suited Simon. Small bladder. Brett weaved her way to the door and pushed it open.

Simon wasn't really used to getting this far. He hoped that his bedroom had the necessary glamour to pull off what was going to happen next. Probably. She stood in the doorway and turned back to him. "Nose blind?" she asked.

"What?" Simon strolled over to her as suavely as he could with his jeans half down and his cock pointing at the ceiling.

"Nose blind," she said again. "It means this room stinks."

Simon stuck his head by her into the room and sniffed. "Of what?"

She shook her head. "Another bedroom?"

Simon shook his head.

YOU'RE LOSING HER. THE SOFA. THE FLOOR. MENTION SOMETHING.

Simon looked at her. "It's that bad?" he asked, his eyebrows raised. She sighed. "What is it?"

"Food," she said. "Like, off food."

Jesus Christ. Under the bed. Kebab. Last night. You fell asleep eating a kebab, right? You pushed it under the bed this morning. Right?

Simon raised his finger in a eureka display, before heading into the room and falling to his knees by the bed. He tossed the sheet back and dragged out an open polystyrene kebab container with half a kofta in it. He sniffed it. Up close he could fucking smell it too. He pulled back, gave her a quick nod and then tossed it out the window. "Howzat?" he asked, displaying a faux cricket swing to boot.

She looked at his cock, swinging freely from his pants and started laughing. "That'll do, pig," she said.

The two of them embraced, and Simon kissed her, passionately. Brett stepped back away from him and pulled the zip down on her dress. She let it drop to the floor. Simon got harder—not something he thought was possible—he could feel himself closer to coming than he should be. She had a fantastic body. Naked under the dress apart from a pair of tight panties.

"Fucking hell," Simon said.

She walked over to him and ran her hand gently over his cock as she passed him and slid onto the bed. She lay there for a moment, running her hands over her body while he watched. She slipped her fingers under the lip of her underwear and closed her eyes as she fingered herself.

Simon was ready to explode.

She smiled and made a sound close to ecstasy, before biting her lip and putting her hands over her head and pushing them under the pillow at her head.

Simon looked at her. She still had her shoes on. She was laid there before him, waiting to be taken. "Brett," he said, quietly. He wanted to touch his cock, but daren't. "Brett?" he said again. She didn't move. "Fuck," he said, a little louder. He reached down and touched her face, gently. "Brittany?" He stood back up right. "She's fucking passed out."

FUCK HER.

"What? No. She's unconscious."

THEN … KILL HER. *THEN* FUCK HER.

Simon was a little stunned at Little Simon's suggestion. Sure, he'd raised ideas about casually murdering people before, but Simon had put that down to it being his own subconscious anger bubbling up to the surface, but the way Little Simon had suggested it this time was different. It was salacious. And she *was* right there. It would be easy, dare he think such a thing. And he did, obviously, otherwise why would Little Simon have said it? Simon reached down to touch Brett's breast. Then he stopped, stealing himself back across the room.

DON'T BE STUPID. DO IT.

"Fuck you, you little prick." Simon turned to the wardrobe and pulled a blanket from on top of it down, and covered Brett.

HOMO.

"Fuck off." Simon pulled his jeans back up and left the room, closing the door gently behind him. He went downstairs, listening to Little Simon telling him what a waste of space he was and how he wished he was someone else's self-doubt. Simon went to the kitchen and grabbed a bottle of Smart Price Whiskey from on top of the cabinet inside the door. Maybe he could drown-out the little shit. He went back to the living room and slumped on the sofa, flicking the TV on with the remote. *Fucking Love Island.* He rolled the cap from the bottle and drunk straight from it. He felt surprisingly sober now, and felt like trying to recreate something of the buzz before he passed out.

C H A P T E R   5

Simon was resting his head on the kitchen table when Brett came downstairs and opened the kitchen door. He sat up and tried to look less like death than he thought he probably did. Little Simon had shut up last night after about half a bottle of whiskey and so far hadn't re-appeared. Brett was wearing her dress again and looked a little sheepish.

"Simon," she said.

He didn't think it was a question, as such, just that she was seeking re-assurance that she wasn't so easy that she didn't remember his name. He nodded and smiled. "Morning," he said. It hurt to smile. Too much whiskey.

"Did we?" She sat down at the table opposite him, letting the question float.

He shook his head. "You blacked out. Coffee?" He started to get up from the table, picking up his own cup to refill it.

She giggled, a little uncomfortably. "Oh, thank God."

Simon snorted. "I'm not that bad am I?" he asked without turning back. That was about right, though. Wake up in a three's house, being an eight, and wondering what the fuck you were thinking. Could have done without the insult though.

"No," she said. "I didn't mean it like that. I just ..." He could hear her shuffling on the chair. "... I just shouldn't hook up when I'm that plastered."

Simon nodded, still unsure. He poured water over the coffee granules, passing a coffee over to her and putting an open bag of sugar on the table. "Help yourself."

"What now?" she asked.

Simon shrugged and sat back down. "I dunno. I never get this far. You tell me."

She looked a little sheepish. "How about I cook you dinner, and make up for all this?"

Simon smiled. Which hurt. "Sounds good." He heard Little Simon waking up.

WHAT HAPPENED?

Simon ignored him. He tried to look at Brett casually, while still being able to appreciate her form. She noticed, he could see, but she didn't say anything. It was … cute. Simon felt suddenly a little warmer on the inside.

Little Simon huffed. This wasn't going to plan.

CHAPTER 6

Simon sat in the pub waiting for Brett. She was running a little late, but she had text. This was their third date, after they'd decided that their first date was dinner at her flat, and not the drunken fumblings of a couple of idiots. That suited him. He was caressing the side of a pint glass, with a little more than half a pint of lager in it, as he sat looking around the pub. It was early, still only just after six, and mostly empty. It was nice, actually waiting for someone who wasn't one of the boys. It felt *normal.*

And Little Simon had been absent a lot over the last couple of weeks. He still made the occasional appearance, but hadn't for a couple of days. Maybe he *was* some manifestation of his self-doubt. It would make some sense. Simon kicked back and watched the two guys at the bar. He wasn't paying them particular attention, it was just where his eyes had rested. They were having some back and forth about something, heated, but friendly. Then one of them noticed him. The dude on the left who was wearing some brown leather fly-boy jacket patted his pal's arm—the second dude was wearing a black leather with tassels. Very nineties. Brown nodded toward Simon and Tassels stopped talking, following his look.

Simon looked away, embarrassed at being caught people watching. They seemed satisfied at him looking away and continued their conversation, albeit a little more subtly. Simon continued to find his own entertainment until Brett appeared, some half an hour—and half a beer—later. She'd gotten caught up at work and had to wait behind for something. Simon got up and greeted her. Pulling her chair out at the table. Gentlemanly, like. Then he went to the bar. She always had vodka tonic, but only a small one. He was solidly off spirits. He ordered at the bar and they sat, talking.

Everything was normal until Brown and Tassels came over, just when the two of them were finishing up and getting ready to leave. They had a table at eight in the Italian around the corner. The two of them stood over the table. It was as intimidating as it was supposed to be.

"Can I help you?" Simon tried to sound normal. Normal was good. Brown stared at Simon without answering and Simon noticed that Tassels was staring at Brett. After a moment's pause, Simon returned his look to Brett suggesting they leave.

"What on earth are you doing with this jackhole?" Tassels directed the question to Brett.

Brett went to stand, nodding to Simon that, *yes, it was time to leave*. Simon slid his chair back, but as Brett went to stand Tassels rested his hand on her shoulder pushing her back into her seat. Simon paused for a second. He didn't want to start a fight. This was all a misunderstanding. Brett looked from Tassels to Simon, and it was clear that Simon should do something with this situation. "Gentleman," he said with authority. "Let me buy you a drink." It worked in the films, after all.

"I don't think so." Brown rested his half empty pint glass down on their table. "I have a drink.

Besides, your whore didn't answer my friend's polite question."

Simon glanced at Brett, and then beyond her to everyone to the bar, hoping to catch the eye of a member of staff. This wasn't a *bouncer* sort of pub, and there was no one there, of course. "Of course," he muttered to himself. Brett looked pissed, understandably. Simon pushed the chair back and stood in a single motion. He couldn't see any other way out of this. Whatever *this* was.

Brown wasn't having any of it though, and said, "Sit, or I shall sit you."

Simon looked from him to Brett, "Come on," he said. "We're leaving."

That was when Brown hit him. He stepped into Simon's space and dug his fist into Simon's gut, causing him to bend forward and then Brown pushed him back into his seat. It took all the wind from Simon, but caused no ruckus. There were no flying chairs, no pool cues being wielded like long swords. As Simon tried to drag the air back into his lungs he looked around the pub. It still wasn't busy but there were people in there, and not a god-damned one of them either noticed, or if they did, stepped in.

Fucking marvellous.

"Arsehole," Brett blurted. She pushed Tassels hand from her shoulder and stood, and Tassels slapped her across the face, pushing her back into her seat.

FUCK HIM UP.

Little Simon spoke for the first time in days, and

was right. Simon knew it. He couldn't let these two toss-pots talk to Brett like that. What sort of man was he? He sucked the air in, and held it in his lungs, the anger finally rising in him. He looked to the side. He wanted a weapon.

GLASS HIM.

Simon grabbed the empty lager glass from the table and smashed the top of it open on the corner of the table. Standing, he could feel the skin on his face tighten as it contorted into a raging scream. He felt like he suddenly had command over the assorted people in the pub, who were now paying attention. He stuck the broken glass into Brown's neck, taking him completely by surprise. He looked moreso when Simon pulled the glass back out and a flurry of blood loosed outwards with a surprising amount of gusto.

It sprayed out with enough force to reach Tassels. Like a Super Soaker.

Brown reached up and cupped the wound. It probably wasn't deep, Simon thought, as he wasn't particularly strong, but it must have hit a vein. *Nice.* Brown was staring at Simon, a look of confusion painted across his face. Simon grinned at him, possibly maniacally.

NUT HIM.

Little Simon was right. Again. And while Simon wasn't thinking about it particularly, something in the back of his mind was nagging him that perhaps they really should hurry up and leave now.

Someone screamed.

Simon glanced at Brett. It wasn't her. He looked

at Tassels, whose face was painted with this mortified and slightly aghast horror. Like he'd picked this sort of fight a thousand times and no one had ever thought to fight back before. Brett pulled her fist back and punched Tassels in the gob while he wasn't paying attention and it had enough force to knock him back, and over a chair. He tumbled to the floor, and someone in the observing crowd whooped. Simon noticed a couple of them fiddling with their phones, and they were about to be on camera. He looked at Brown, still clutching his neck and launched his forehead into his nose. There was sickening crack and more blood than Simon had ever seen suddenly waterfalled out of his face. He went down like a sack of shit and was left lying on the sticky carpet squirming, blood running from the wound on his neck, out from under his hand.

Simon reached across and took Brett's hand. "Come on, Bonnie," he said, guiding her around Tassels and then Brown.

"Coming, Clyde."

The two of them bolted for the door. Simon could hear the barman who had conveniently returned now that the deed was done, calling after them. *They couldn't leave. The police had to be called. An ambulance.* Simon pushed the door open and let Brett out first, then gave a cheeky salute to the crowd, the cameras, and they were gone.

Around the corner they ran towards the town. "Oh my God," Brett was saying. "You were amazing. My fucking hero."

The two of them ran hand in hand across the old

town and through the pedestrianised area. Simon felt great. He felt alive. Apart from the cut on his hand where he'd sliced himself on the glass. And that his head hurt. He really needed to find out how you were supposed to *nut* someone.

"You are having the best sex tonight," Brett squealed.

Simon led Brett around another corner and on to a hill. They hurried up and around another corner. And another. Soon they were in the middle of the high street, a mile away from the pub, and yet in the distance they could still hear the sirens. He looked at her, grinning like a madman. Then he kissed her.

CHAPTER 7

Brett laid on her front with her arse in the air and Simon pushed himself as far as his girth would allow in, and then back. Not all the way out, but enough that her pussy would pucker to hold onto him. Each time he did, he could hear her sigh in satisfaction. But he knew he couldn't keep this up for too long though. He was already ready to blow.

I CAN HELP.

Simon ignored him, keeping his eyes tightly shut.

REALLY. I SAW A CAT IN THE ALLEYWAY DOWN THE SIDE OF THE PUB WHEN YOU WERE BOLTING IT LIKE A CHICKEN SHIT. IT HAD PUS RUNNING FROM IT'S FACE. IT HAD BEEN HIT BY A CAR BY THE LOOK OF IT. BROKEN LEG. ALL OUT OF WHACK. FUCKING THING WILL BE DEAD BY NOW. FOXES'LL HAVE IT. TEAR ITS SKIN OFF AND CHOW ON THE FLESH BENEATH. FOXES EAT THE BRAINS OF CATS. DID YOU KNOW THAT? ANYWAY. THE CORPSE WILL ROT THERE, IN THAT ALLEYWAY, REMEMBER? FOR A FEW DAYS AT LEAST. IT'LL STINK IT UP. THE GUY WHO OWNS THE PUB—THE ONE THAT DIDN'T CALL THE POLICE WHEN YOU WERE BEING PICKED ON LIKE A BITCH—HE'LL CALL THE COUNCIL ON THE CAT CORPSE. THEY'LL SEND A ROAD SWEEPER PROBABLY. THEN HE'LL PICK UP WHAT'S LEFT OF THE CORPSE. HE'LL SPIKE IT WITH THAT SPIKE ON A STICK THEY USE FOR PICKING UP CRISP BAGS IN THE STREET SO THEY DON'T HAVE TO BEND DOWN. HE'LL PROBABLY HOLD IT UP, TRYING TO WORK OUT WHAT THE FUCK IT WAS NOW IT'S JUST A ROTTEN LUMP

OF PUS RIDDEN FLESH. A *PUS*-Y PUSSY. HEH. GET IT?
SPEAKING OF WHICH, HOW'S THE TIGHT ONE, HERE?
ANY PUS IN HER PUSSY? NOT YET I SEE, BUT YOU'RE
WORKING ON IT. SEE WHAT I DID THERE? PUS? CUM?
DISCHARGE, YES. YOU MISSED YOUR TABLE AT THE
ITALIAN. YOU MUST BE HUNGRY. HAVING FISH
TONIGHT? BOOM-BOOM. NAH. I DON'T SUPPOSE YOU
WANT TO LICK YOUR OWN DISCHARGE FROM THE FISH,
RIGHT? OR DO YOU? YOU HAVE BEEN A RIGHT BITCH
UP UNTIL NOW. CUCK, MUCH.

Simon grunted as he got closer. Brett was saying
cum in me, over and over, as she shuddered
orgasming hard.

DAMN IT YOU'RE A SICK FUCK. GONNA BLOW
YOUR LOAD IN HER CUNT WHILE I TALK ABOUT CATS
THAT HAVE HAD THEIR FLESH TORN OFF THEM? DOES
THAT TURN YOU ON? DID I MISJUDGE YOU? I WAS
TALKING SICK SHIT TO HELP YOU OUT, NOT MAKE YOU
CUM FASTER. WELL. I SUPPOSE YOU OUGHT TO BE
THINKING ABOUT REALLY WEIRD SHIT WHEN YOU CUM,
THEN SICKO. WHAT'S NEXT IN THAT HEAD OF YOURS?
THINKING ABOUT FUCKING THE DEAD CAT? HOLDING
IT'S STILL WARM FLESH AROUND YOUR COCK LIKE A
FLESHLIGHT? POUNDING ON IT. PUS FOR LUBE?

Simon exploded inside Brett, and she squealed
with delight. As he shuddered to a stop, he pulled
himself out, and rolled onto the bed next to her.
"Jesus Christ," she said. She twisted around onto her
side and lifted one leg up. "What have you been
doing, storing it up since winter?" She rolled off the
bed, and slapped Simon's leg gently. "Shower." She
got up and hurried out of the room.

Simon lay there, drooping. He panted trying to

get his breath back. He pulled the rubber off, and tossed it under the edge of the bed.

You see. Together we're better.

Simon turned over and pulled his boxers off the sheets, wiping his cock off with them, tossing them over to the other side of the room, before he pulled the sheets up over himself and lay back on the pillow. He listened to the shower turn on, and Brett's squee when she dived under the water too quickly and it was still cold.

When you did what I said, she liked it.

Simon listened to her shower. He was warming under the sheet. The weather was getting cooler, but he hadn't bothered to put the heating on yet. He heard the shower go off. Briefly he wondered if she was going to find a clean towel in there. Then he remembered putting one out that morning. More luck than judgement. He heard her piss real quick—the house was built in the fifties and walls were real thin—then he heard her leave the bathroom and pad down the hall. He held the sheet up and she jumped in the bed next to him, snuggling together.

"You're the best," she said. "That was the best. Like, ever."

You hear that? She had the best sex ever. You wouldn't have gotten her hot like that with me telling you what to do, would you? You wouldn't have lasted as long without me. She wouldn't have finished. You'd have disappointed her. Like you do everyone.

Admit it.

YOU'RE A BETTER YOU WHEN I'M HELPING.

Simon stood in the hallway outside the office of someone called *Trevor*. Trevor had a name plaque on the door that just said Trevor. Just from that, Simon could tell he was one of those bosses who tried to be *one of the team*. Someone who thought that he could be friends with the rest of the staff and that they would treat him so.

Twat.

What made him more of a twat was that on Wednesdays Simon had to vacuum out the offices of *Airport Shuttles*, the company that rented the third floor, left hand side of Kings House, and he was still in his office. The door was open and when Simon had gone to enter the office—making that oh so polite gentle fake knock on the already open door—Trevor had waved his mobile phone at him and motioned for him to wait outside. It was already gone six and he hadn't gotten to the toilets yet.

"Ya. Ya," he was saying.

He sounded like a right plonker, reminding Simon of the TV character, Alan Partridge.

"Okay, Heathrow. Four-thirty? Two. No problem." He tossed the phone on the desk and beckoned Simon in. "Hey, hey."

Who did he think he was, Crusty? Simon entered the office, pulling the vacuum behind him. "Just need to ..." he muttered and didn't finish his sentence. It was blatantly fucking obvious what he was doing. He pulled the waste bin out from under the back of the desk and took it out into the hall tipping it into a bin liner. When he returned to Trevor's office, Trevor was pulling his suit jacket on.

"I'm out." He looked at Simon and smiled. When he smiled his nose pushed his glasses up a little and he looked stupid. "Have a good night." He ran his hand over his head, half covered in hair with a hairline so far receded that it made his forehead the size of Telecom Tower.

"Okay," Simon responded, unsure what the twat wanted from him.

Then he left. Simon watched him leave the office and then quickly plugged in the vacuum cleaner. He turned it on and stuck his head out the door, making sure Trevor was actually leaving. He had a date with Brett tonight and didn't want to hang around here. Trevor pulled open the front door of the main office and disappeared through. Simon picked up the nozzle of the vacuum and ran it over the carpet in front of Trevor's desk, then switched the cleaner off. He unplugged it and coiled the cable around his arm, picking up the cleaner and the bin liner on his way out.

Simon went to the cleaner's closet next to the toilets and dropped off the vacuum, tossing the bin liner in the corner. He could deal with that tomorrow. He just needed to do the toilets now, and that was an easy fix: just flush them and spray the air freshener. It would do, just this once. He took the spray can and went into the ladies, knocking once, as per the company handbook, and went from cubicle to cubicle flushing each of the toilets and giving a quick spray.

He looked at his watch. Six twenty. He was doing okay for time.

Simon left the ladies, crossed the front of the lifts and went into the gents.

As soon as he opened the door he knew that this wasn't going to be good. The stench of something noxious punched him in the nose. It smelt like something had crawled up someone's arsehole and died. *It made his eyes water.*

The bolt on the inside of the middle cubicle made the unmistakable clack, and the door opened. *Trevor.*

He looked at Simon and nodded, then strode over to the sinks, looking himself in the mirror. He started to fuss with his hair.

Simon watched him from the corner of his eye. He didn't wash his hands before touching his face, so he can't have just … can he? Simon walked over to the first cubicle and pushed the door open. He looked down into the bowl. Empty. Clean enough, too. He pushed the flush on the cistern with the base of the air freshener. He came out and looked at the back of Trevor's head. He was trying to smooth his hair, by licking his fingers and smearing his own spit on the back of his head, like a child's mum. Simon went into the middle cubicle. The smell was appalling in there. The shit had somehow managed to create humidity in the air. "Fucking hell," he muttered. He glanced down the bowl and looked at the shit that Trevor had left there. He turned and looked at him.

I CAN FEEL HOW ANGRY YOU ARE.

He was. Simon was on the knife edge of losing his shit. For this, this, arsehat to look him in the eye and acknowledge him when he'd walked out of a cubicle without flushing his shit like a fucking animal.

HE'LL DO IT AGAIN. IT WAS PROBABLY HIM LAST TIME. *IT WILL BE HIM NEXT TIME.*

Simon clenched his fingers around the metal freshener can. He didn't move. He just watched Trevor. Trevor sighed, and finally turned on the tap and made his fingers wet, before trying his hair, again. "There's blood in your stool," said Simon. Trevor's hand stopped moving, like he knew that Simon was talking to him, but was going to pretend he hadn't heard anything. "*Trevor*," Simon snapped at him. He saw Trevor physically jump. It's not like Simon was some tramp on the midnight underground asking him for cash. Twat.

Trevor turned, and pretended. "I'm sorry, are you talking to me?"

Simon sighed. He stepped to the side of the toilet and pointed down into the bowl. "There's blood in there. That's a bad sign."

Trevor looked unsure, squinting at Simon through his spectacles. He stepped forward, every movement and motion, his body language, belaying fake confusion. What was happening? Why are you talking to me? Stool? Blood? What are these things you bother me with? But he walked over. Simon could see that behind his eyes his fear and trepidation over being cornered by the cleaner had been overcome by the possibility of there being blood in his shit.

And everybody knew that meant cancer.

He scurried, hunched, past Simon and into the

cubicle looking down into the bowl.

It was all that Simon needed to push him over the edge. He knew that nobody—especially this jumped up little prick—would stick their head down a toilet in this shit stanking bathroom, unless it was their own shit down there.

Trevor leaned forward. "Where?"

Simon grabbed the back of the twat's hair and thrust him forward into the pool of faeces, piss included. He hit his forehead—because it was so large—on the porcelain at the back of the bowl, before the dunk itself. Trevor started to thrash. He had no balance, and collapsed further down even than Simon had pushed him. He grabbed the sides of the toilet and pushed against Simon, heaving a great gulp of air as he managed to get above the water line. He wasn't strong—in fact with the given leverage Simon managed to push him down into the pool of floaters with some ease. The shit water bubbled around his face as he struggled to stay calm enough to try and hold his breath. Simon held him there. See the shit. Feel the shit. Trevor struggled, and Simon thought to let him up. He had no real intention of actually killing the dirty bastard.

DROWN HIM. DROWN. HIM.

"What?" Simon relaxed slightly, letting Trevor up for air.

MAKE HIM PAY.

Little Simon's voice rasped. Simon could tell that he was enjoying the show. The release of anger. "No," Simon said, letting Trevor go completely. Trevor pushed himself so hard backwards he fell from the cubicle, onto his arse and he scooted back across the floor of the bathroom until his back met the pipework underneath the sinks. He had a clump of his own crap stuck to his mortified face. His mouth was contorted into utter disgust and glasses, gone. Lost to the sea of shit. Blood ran from a cut on his forehead, running down his face, blending with the brown water across his face. He swiped at his skin with the back of his jacket sleeve, still without word. He slipped on the wet floor—mostly his own piss, Simon assumed—as he tried to get to his feet, dragging himself up by the sinks that stood proud of the wall above him, until he was looking at Simon in the mirror as he faced them.

He glanced from Simon to his own face, now smeared with shit from the pathetic sleeve swipe. "You're going to pay for that," he said, keeping his eyes on Simon, who hadn't moved. "I'll have your job. Press charges. You're a crazy man."

HE'S RIGHT. HE'LL PRESS CHARGES. THE POLICE WILL TAKE YOU AWAY.

He turned on the tap and stuck his hands under the running cold water—it took nearly five minutes for the hot water to reach the taps in this bathroom. Then he cupped his hands under the water and splashed it onto his face bending forward as he did, then standing again quickly, watching Simon.

YOU'LL BE A CRIMINAL. BRETT WILL LEAVE YOU.

Simon looked around the cubicle. He couldn't let that happen. His heart beat quicker. He had to stop it. His stomach clenched. He returned his look to Trevor, still watching him in the mirror. "I-I …"

"What?"

"I didn't mean to. I lost my temper."

Trevor turned his head back to look directly at Simon. "You're going to lose a lot more than that." The words seemed to pacify Trevor and take some of his fear. "You need help." He turned back and started to fill his hands with water again.

STOP HIM.

Simon grabbed the top of the cistern and pulled off the two-foot long piece of porcelain. It was heavy. Solid. He walked up behind Trevor, bent over the sink, holding the cistern lid from each side. He stood behind him and raised it up, just as Trevor looked up, from his hands, into the mirror. The two of them silently appraised each other, neither moving. And just as Trevor was going to say something, Simon brought the porcelain weapon down onto the back of his head.

The lid didn't break, but pitched into Trevor's skull with surprising ease. Simon wasn't really expecting anything, he wasn't thinking, but had expected some friction in the collision, but there was next to none. The porcelain smashed through Trevor's head, spraying blood up the mirror, and crashing into his brain.

Simon just stood there, somewhat shocked. He was still holding the lid with it impaled into Trevor's head, and the two of them met eyes again. Well, Simon's eyes to Trevor's *eye*, singular, as the other had been pushed out of its socket by the pressure, and was only attached to his head now by a stringy bit of optic malarkey that Simon didn't know the name of.

After all the splashing and accusations, and the

cracking sound of the bone shattering, the bathroom was now misted in a pleasant quietness.

Apart from the sound of Trevor's brain matter dripping into the sink.

CHAPTER 9

"What have I done?" Simon still hadn't moved. He had been holding onto the porcelain now for what felt like an eternity. He forced his fingers open and released his grip, stepping back from the body. He jumped when it twitched.

HEH. PROBABLY STILL ALIVE. *TECHNICALLY.*

"How can you say that?" Simon looked at his hands. There was blood splatter on them. He heard dripping. It was louder than before. There was blood still pumping, albeit slowly now, from Trevor's head. It was running down the side of his skull, bypassing the sink and onto his shoulder, down his arm and flowing onto the rubber resin waterproof floor. It was pooling outwards towards him. He backed into the cubicle away from the mess. Away from the guilt. "Oh God. I need to call an ambulance."

TOO LATE FOR THAT.

"What do you mean?" Simon glanced to his side, failing to see Little Simon. "I've got to do something."

I THINK YOU'VE ALREADY DONE SOMETHING.

"I'm going to jail." Simon sat down on the toilet, staring at Trevor as he twitched his last, more blood on the floor now than in inside his body.

NOT NECESSARILY.

"What do you mean?"

JUST DO AS I SAY. WHEN HAVE I EVER LED YOU ASTRAY?

Simon had sent Brett a text first. Cover your tracks. *Someone's made a mess in the toilets. Going to be an hour late x*, he had sent. He wondered if the kiss was too much? It's not like he'd sent her undying love, right? He was on his hands and knees in the toilet. He had removed and cleaned the cistern lid and replaced it behind the toilet. There was a hairline crack in it, but unless forensics were in here—and if they were he would probably be fucked anyway—there was no way anyone was seeing it. He'd scrubbed the back of the toilet, and in it, getting rid of all evidence of the scuffle, and anything that suggested Trevor had been there to start with. He had retrieved Trevor's glasses and tucked them into his pocket for safe keeping.

He kept looking over at the body on the floor of the bathroom, its head caved in.

Simon scrubbed.

He dragged the body across the floor of the bathroom and out into the hall. A polythene sheet from the cleaner's cupboard covered the floor. He pulled Trevor onto it and carefully wrapped the sheet around the body, tying off each end and pushing him into the cleaners cupboard—no more sizeable than a closet—so that he could get out of the building.

He was the last one in there tonight. Luckily.

By the time he'd gotten himself cleaned up and checked himself thoroughly in the mirror, getting to the doors to the building, he found them locked. He fished through his pockets. He had a front door key to the building that he rarely used. Outside, he locked the door back up. No one alarmed the building. Ever. It wasn't something that Simon had thought was a good idea, but equally, he never heard that there had been a break in, either.

But it was just as well.

Simon ran across the bridge. He pulled the phone from his pocket and looked at the time. He was over an hour late already. He dialled the local taxi firm and asked for a cab from the bus stop.

The cab arrived less than five minutes later and he hopped in, giving the driver his address. Brett was waiting for him at his place.

Simon ran up the path to the house and stabbed the key into the lock, just as Brett opened the door from the inside. "I saw you coming," she said. She smiled, warmly. He hoped that meant she wasn't pissed about how late he was. He'd sent a text only a few minutes ago from the back of the cab apologising again.

"I'm really sorry," he said—*again*. "I just had so much to do."

She embraced him and kissed him deeply. "Don't worry," she said as they parted. "Dinner's ready."

Simon smiled. "Shower," he said, pointing up the stairs.

"Be quick." She pecked him on the cheek and headed towards the kitchen.

Simon bounded up the stairs and went straight into the bathroom, closing the door and locking it. He switched the shower on and the water pumped out cold. "I'm never going to get away with this," he said. "Fucking murder."

YOU'LL BE FINE. YOU'RE DOING A STERLING JOB.

Little Simon sounded different. He sounded … thoughtful.

Simon was poking around under his finger nails. "Gross," he whispered, scraping bits of Trevor out. He pulled his shirt off and tossed it into the laundry basket under the sink. Same with his trousers and pants. Then he showered. He was surprised at how red the water ran, even though he'd cleaned himself so thoroughly. Hopefully the taxi drive didn't notice anything amiss.

He dried himself off and went naked along to the bedroom where he dressed in clean clothes. He set out an old ripped pair of jeans and a black t-shirt for later, and then he went downstairs to eat with Brett.

CHAPTER 10

Simon sat on the edge of the bed looking at the clock. It was just after one in the morning. He felt terrible that he'd had to fake sickness and get Brett a taxi home just after eleven, but she seemed okay with it. More worried about him, she had said. But he needed her out of the way. "This is never going to work."

TRUST ME.

Simon dressed in the clothes that he set out earlier and left the house on foot. His parents lived on the other side of the estate and he was going to get their car.

The estate was a ropey place at the best of times, and his parents still lived in one of the worst areas. He just hoped that at this time of night there might be less people on the streets.

Simon would normally cross the road in plenty of time to avoid any sort of contact with other people on the street. The lone walker didn't usually both him. He felt that he could always take care of himself when there was just one of them, but when there were two or more, he didn't feel that he was *that* handy in a fight to be able to win. He dare not risk it. Previously, when he saw a group of two or more coming towards him a knot would tie in his stomach. Even after crossing the street, he would dwell on what to say if they spoke to him. It was the sort of place that they would jeer at him and call him names, knowing that if he was on his own he would do nothing in retaliation—and that sort of shit, he could do without.

If they had wanted to take something from him, they could. Even his clothes—which had never happened to him before, but was something he had heard about. There was nothing he could do about it.

But that was before.

He still crossed the street when he saw someone coming though. On the short walk he cross three times: twice for a lone walker, and one for a duo of them. He crossed when he saw the duo coming and as they got closer he saw that it was a young couple, probably on their way home from a club. They weren't likely to be a problem. And tonight he was buoyed on by what had happened earlier. It was like someone had found a switch inside of him, and though they hadn't flicked it—not yet, anyway—they were teasing it. He felt more confident. Stronger.

Simon turned into his parent's road. The car was sitting on the other side of the street. It was old, and a little beaten up. Every car on the estate ended up a little beaten up after a while. There were no driveways in most of the front gardens—apart from the big arse house at the end of the street—so the cars got dings and scratches from the kids playing football in the road and the drunks coming home in the middle of the night.

Still. It was his father's pride and joy.

He turned up his parent's path and went down the side of the house, stepping over the fallen fence between theirs and next doors as quietly as he could. Around the back of the house he tried the back door which was locked. Good. As it should be. On occasion he had found that they were going to bed and leaving the door unlocked by accident. He'd spoken to them as gently as he could, trying hard not to lose his temper. Leaving your doors unlocked on this estate got you robbed ... or worse.

He pulled his keys from his pocket and unlocked the door. They didn't have a spare front door key, so this was the one he got. It suited him then, and it suited him now. He slipped silently into the kitchen. On a key rack inside the back door was every key to everything. He clenched his fist around the set of keys for the car so that they didn't jangle when he moved them and he took them.

Back out, locking the door behind him. He took the car.

CHAPTER 11

Simon drove into the basement parking moat of King's House. He pulled to a stop at the basement entrance, and killed the engine, turning the lights off. "You still with me?" he asked. There was a nervous catch in his voice.

I AM.

"Is this going to work?" He rounded the back of the car and opened the boot. It was empty as he expected it to be. Good ol' man. If it had been his old car—a second hand Mondeo that he'd picked up cheap, the boot would have been full of rubbish waiting to be dropped off at the tip, or at someone's house. He closed the boot quietly, looking around to make sure he hadn't gotten anyone's attention. It was gone two now, but it was mid-week so the streets were mostly empty. Mostly. He locked the car.

IT IS. TRUST ME. WE CAN—*YOU*—CAN DO THIS.

Simon went over to the staff entrance in the car park and unlocked it. In, he locked the door again and hit the button for the lift, but left the lights off. No sense in advertising his presence. *Bing*. The doors opened. When they closed after he was in, and the lift had started towards the third floor a small weight lifted. He felt a little safer now, locked in the building. *Bing*. The doors slid open and Simon got out. Here on the third floor he was higher than most of the buildings around him. He stayed away from the windows so as not to be seen, but he stood and looked out for a moment. He was telling himself that he was keeping a watch, but deep down he was just delaying the inevitable. Seeing the body again.

WE'RE NEARLY OUT THE WOODS. JUST A LITTLE WHILE LONGER.

Simon nodded. He took a breath, still keeping his eyes on the window, and then he crossed the small lobby to the cleaner's cupboard. He opened the door, half expecting the stench of death—whatever that might be—to come flooding over him, but instead it was just the usual smell of the cupboard … a bleachy, soapy, smell.

He stared at the polythene. It wasn't thick enough to hide Trevor's features beneath it. He could see his one eyed death stare looking at him through the plastic. His other eye wasn't attached anymore, probably torn from the nerves when he moved the body. But he hadn't seen it about anywhere when he was tidying—he was sure he would have noticed—and so knew that it must still be in the folds of the plastic somewhere. He picked up the end of the polythene sheet and dragged Trevor out in to the lobby. He pressed the lift button and the doors slid open, the lift unmoved.

Simon pulled the body in and pressed the button to return to the basement.

The lift clunked as it started to move, and Simon stared at Trevor. He watched as the corpse lolled in the plastic with the jerky movement of the antiquated lift.

I FEEL GOOD ABOUT THIS.

Simon nodded. He didn't. At all. But Little Simon was right. He'd go to jail forever for this.

Bing. The doors trundled open and Simon stepped out. He went over to the door into the car park and made sure there was no one out there. The coast clear, he pulled Trevor from the lift and out to the rear of the car.

He put him in the boot, making sure that the blood stayed inside the polystyrene. Getting in, he drove around the moat and back out onto the road. He drove down through the town and out to the harbour. Beyond that, he rode the hill to the top of the cliffs and along as far as the road took him, stopping eventually at the park at the end of the cliffs. *George IV Memorial Park*. Simon parked in the gated entrance. It still wasn't three. He got Trevor out of the boot and slung him over his shoulder. Little Simon was muttering some words of encouragement quietly, as Simon huffed, getting the dead weight onto him and maintaining his balance. He carried him into the park and along the tree line that met the cliff tops. There were signs all the way along. *Beware. Unmarked Edge*. Simon squinted through the darkness gently feeling forward with his feet until he could hear the crashing of the waves on the rocks below.

YOU KNOW, SOMEONE SHOULD PUT A FENCE UP HERE. THIS IS FUCKING DANGEROUS.

Simon let out a quick laugh. Even he was surprised by it. "Quite," he said. He firmed his footing and hefted Trevor over his head and down in front of him, near the edge. He opened the plastic, and sat with Trevor's body between him and the drop, then used his feet to roll him from the plastic, onto the grass, and over the edge. Simon released a guttural sound like he was going to be sick. He sat there for a moment. There was a feeling of relief that came with Trevor's disappearance over the edge. Simon got to his knees and gathered up the polythene.

He stood and tossed it over the edge into the wind, watching as it disappeared into the darkness, carried on the air.

Even though the night was still, a sound like the rumble of thunder rolled over the water. Simon looked out. "What was that?"

NOTHING.

Simon shook his head, and made his way back to the car. He tried to see if he was bloody as he stalked through the dimly lit park. Pretty clean, he returned the car to his parents and dropped off the keys. They would never know he had been there.

Then he went home.

It was nearly four when his head hit the pillow.

Little Simon sat and watched him, his eyes slowly coming to a close. He was doing well.

CHAPTER 1 2

Simon opened his eyes and stared at the ceiling of his bedroom. There was water. Not like the roof of the house was leaking, but water. He tried to focus in on it, but couldn't, like his mind refused to acknowledge what his eyes were telling it. The ocean roared above him in the room.

The smell of salt pricked at his nose. A cold breeze raised goose bumps on his arms, and he gripped his sheets in his fists justifying that he was still in his bed. He looked around and the walls were disappearing, fading into the gloom. He pushed himself up on his elbows. "I'm just dreaming," he said. He went to swing his feet from the bed to the floor, but the rocking of water, the sickness that it brought, it made him stay, balanced precariously on the bed. He caught sight of his right arm. Welts and sores covered it, the skin broken apart, and calloused.

His breathing was laboured.

"It's just a dream," he shouted, punching himself in the chest, trying to wake himself. The bed rocked as the water on the ceiling swelled, disorienting him further.

There was something moving under the current above him.

Simon pulled the sheets up against him like a child hiding from the bogeyman.

The movement seemed to go on for all eternity as if below the water's shroud the thing was as big as the universe. It covered the width of the room, and then beyond. It dipped out below the surface of the water, into the room above Simon just once for him to see the smooth grey skin of the thing. It wasn't something that Simon had ever witnessed before, not even in his own mind. He cowered on the bed, his mind racing, asking how he could create something of such monstrosity from his own imagination, when it sunk, up, below the water again. "Wake up," he cried. "I didn't mean to." His voice dropped to a whimper as he curled on his bed. The guilt that caused the nightmare drowning him where he lay. "I didn't mean to …"

The monster of his guilt disappeared above the roiling waters, away from sight.

Simon held onto the bed, nausea gripping his stomach, burning in his throat. He could feel the pain in his flesh start to creep, pushing past the numbness created by the cold. His skin was pale, and bereft of life, crinkled, and wrinkled, and cracked.

Pain shot from his other arm, and he saw the word burning itself onto his skin.

The word was *coming*.

CHAPTER 13

"You look like crap on a stick," Brett said. She grinned at Simon and pushed by him to get into the house. It was only eight in the morning. She'd stopped in on her way into work to see if he was feeling better. His lack of sleep seeming to solidify his excuse. "Whatcha doing today? I brought you soup." She opened her handbag and pulled out a can of Campbell's Condensed.

"Uh, thanks." He closed the door and followed her through. "I've got to do some shopping before work tonight."

"Cool." She pecked him on the cheek. "Look after yourself and go to the chemist if you start to feel like shit." She slapped him on the arse and headed for the front door. "See you tonight?"

"Yeah, sure." He still had one eye partially shut, possibly glued together with that green shit that comes from nowhere during sleep. "No problem." She closed the door, the house falling into silence. Simon put the kettle on and made a coffee.

SO WHAT ARE WE DOING?

"What do you mean?"

WELL, AFTER LAST NIGHT. YOU MUST BE AMPED, KILLER.

"Don't call me that." Simon sipped the coffee. "You heard. I'm going into town for a while."

NO PROBLEM. I'LL JUST KEEP TO MYSELF. I KNOW

WHEN I'M NOT WANTED.

"Clearly not."

Simon got dressed and hit the streets about eleven. He'd really liked to have gone back to bed for a while, but he had to get out, and in the house, in the silence, Little Simon tended to suddenly fill the void.

He walked off the estate and onto the main road, getting a bus down into town.

Sitting in the window, on the top deck of the bus, he watched the helicopter circling. He couldn't tell what it was for sure, but he knew why it was there.

They'd already found him.

He stayed on the bus as it rounded the town, ready to get off at the harbour. He listened to Little Simon the whole time. He was muttering. Sometimes it was intelligible, sometimes not. He was belittling Simon, taunting him. He was calling him names. But not directly, just … there. In the back of his head.

As the bus pulled up at the harbour stop, Simon grabbed the metal pole on the bus and dragged himself to his feet, steadying himself. He walked down to the front, along with almost everyone else, and got out onto the path.

Little Simon was still there.

He tried to block it out by humming to himself. He should have brought something to listen to. But

Little Simon was there, over the top. Audible. Always.

The police presence in the town was high. There were cars going back and forth, mostly heading in the direction of the park. Simon crossed the road and into the high street. He browsed some of the windows while making his way towards the small supermarket there.

Stood, looking in the window of the bakery, he wondered if he should go in and get a sausage roll. The small bakers sold coffee and a bacon butty for a pound, but he'd had it once and it was a gross as the price would suggest it would be.

THERE.

Simon ignored him.

THERE.

"What?" he snapped, barely audibly.

LOOK IN THE REFLECTION. TASSELS.

Simon looked around the street in the reflection of the glass in the shop window and sure enough on the other side of the street was Tassels.

YOU SHOULD MAKE HIM PAY FOR WHAT HE DID TO BRITTANY.

Simon watched him. He was shambling about, not doing anything in particular. He looked tantamount to homeless. He was dressed the same as before. Maybe he hadn't even changed? *It's been while, though.* An old woman came and stood next to Simon to look in the window.

YOU REMEMBER HOW HARD SHE FUCKED YOU

"Don't be fucking stupid."

The old woman looked from the display to Simon. "It's only sausage rolls," she said, shaking her head and ducking into the shop. Simon watched her. She went in and straight to the counter where she pointed through the glass to him. The young woman behind the counter turned and stared at him. He gave a half-hearted wave and then turned back into the street. The wind was up and he hunched his shoulders.

Tassels was nearly at the centre of the pedestrian area, and crossing to continue up the street.

Simon looked from him to the supermarket on the corner and then back again. He decided to follow Tassels up the street. Something, somewhere in the back of his mind thought it was a good idea. Something that was making him very tired.

CHAPTER 14

Simon followed Tassels at a fair distance as he moseyed his way up the high street and out the top into a rundown part of the town that was mostly old Victorian houses converted into flats. The sort of places that had their front doors around the backs of the property, up alleyways full of trash. Alleys that stank like piss and vomit.

Flats that normal decent people didn't want to stay in.

Simon watched Tassels as he turned up a side street, and then ran to the corner to watch him. Each time he thought about stopping and going back to the supermarket, something compelled him to just know a little more … to follow him just a little further.

Something that was clouding his judgement.

From the corner of the street he watched him take a right down the side of a long abandoned paper shop. Simon followed. Tassels was standing up the side of the shop fiddling with his keys. He looked like he might have already been drinking. He seemed to find what he was looking for in his hands and then went down the steps to the basement of the shop. He fumbled again and used the keys to open the door.

Simon was now watching him from the top of the steps. He wasn't even hiding anymore. He wanted to know what was in there, though.

Tassels realised that someone was watching him—a sixth sense—or some such, and he turned and looked. It was definitely him. Simon had his face etched onto his brain, but Tassels almost looked through him. There was no sense of recollection in his eyes at all.

It was apparent that he wasn't drunk. Whatever Tassels had been doing this morning was far stronger than alcohol. "What?" he shouted at Simon.

Simon shook his head. He was a pathetic sight. A wreck of a man. A waste of the skin he was in. "You don't remember me?"

Tassels squinted at him. He was wavering slightly like a drunk peeing up against a wall. He shook his head and pushed the door open, his attention turned away from Simon. Apparently the conversation was over, as he stumbled into the flat.

Simon went down the steps and looked in the front door. Tassels was just inside, fighting to get his jacket off in the small hallway of the basement flat. He turned, jacket half off, and looked at him in surprise. "What do you want?"

"To be adored," Simon replied. His eyes glazed over black as night, and a rumble that sounded like thunder rolled across the sky. He pushed his way in through the door, grabbing Tassels by the jacket lapels, and pushing him further into the darkness of the flat.

Tassels screamed out. "Help me," he shouted.

"No one will hear you," said Simon. He could suddenly hear everything. He could suddenly feel everything. He felt like he was at one with the world itself. And he no longer cared that he wasn't in control.

He pushed Tassels down the hallway, past a pushbike leaning against the wall and off his feet. The man crumpled to the floor, flailing like a fool.

Simon turned back and closed the front door quietly, before returning his attention to Tassels. "You hurt me," he said. He could feel the slap he gave Brett like he *was* Brett.

Tassels crawled backwards. He had tears welling in his eyes. "I don't know you." The words came out a whine.

"Pathetic." Simon walked over to him, standing over him. "Pathetic fool," he said. Simon raised his foot up and stomped on Tassels lower arm. He screamed out as it twisted, pushed against the hallway wall.

"What are you doing?" he wailed.

Simon stomped again. Harder. The same place. There was snap. It cut through the silence of the flat, broken only by the pathetic cries of the man on the floor. The snap was the man's ulna bone. Simon knew which bone it was. He knew everything now. Tassels screamed in pain. He clutched at his arm. He was looking around like a cornered animal. Partly paralysed in fear, but partly desperate to escape. Simon bent forwards over him and took him again by the lapels. He dragged him to his feet, a feat far beyond his normal strength. Tassels wasn't big, but even Simon knew he shouldn't be able to pick him up. He dragged him through the flat to the kitchen.

It was filthy. A stink rose from every corner. Food discarded to the floor. A table stood in the middle of the room. Old. Beaten up.

Simon tossed Tassels onto it like he was a tablecloth. He crashed onto the table shrieking out in pain, for help, trying to get someone's attention. Still he cradled his arm. "Please," he begged, laying on the table staring at the ceiling. "I don't know what you want."

Simon stood over him, his hand placed on Tassels chest as he lay there, the simple gesture enough to stop Tassels from moving. "I want to be adored by her," he said.

The man just looked confused. "Who?" he asked quietly.

BRETT.

Tassels was still confused. "I don't—"

"You won't." Simon grasped Tassels good wrist and pulled it across the table. He reached down and undid the man's belt with one hand, pulling it from his jeans. It was easy. Tassels was sloppy and his clothes didn't fit right. Simon then used the belt to restrain his hand to the corner of the table—around the leg. He tried clawing at the belt, but his broken arm stopped him. He just cried and wailed and screamed in pain and fear. Simon smiled. He pulled the cord form the kettle and the wall and yanked Tassels broken arm back, crucifying him on the table and tying him off just like it. He walked around the kitchen. Simon pulled open drawers and cabinets, taking anything he felt he might use. He dropped knives to the counter top. Bottle openers. He found bleach. Under the sink was a container of liquid and when Simon twisted off the lid and smelt it, it was petrol. He put in on the counter. "What's your name?" he mused as he searched.

Tassels just cried, making indistinguishable noises.

Simon turned back to him and slammed his hands, palm flat, onto the table.

Tassels stopped.

"Name?" he demanded.

"M-Matthew," he said. "Who are you?"

WE ARE SIMON.

CHAPTER 15

Matthew wept as Simon wandered the kitchen, then the flat. He wasn't looking for anything in particular. He just wanted to drag out the anticipation of the act. Little Simon wanted it. *Needed it.* When he came back into the kitchen Matthew hadn't moved. He had his head on its side and was staring at his arm, purple bruising coming up and the bone jutting out, but not piercing the skin. He was breathing hard. Laboured. He was scared.

As he should be.

Simon went over to the counter top where he had left all the tools that he had found. "Do you know how long it will be before you are found here?"

"What do you mean?" Matthew sobbed between words.

"Your dead body. Your death. Do you know how long it will be before you are found after I kill you?"

"They'll be home soon." He was wheezing. Fear. "They'll be home any minute. If you leave now, you can still get away."

Simon looked at the wall above the cooker. The cooker was grimy. The wall above it somehow worse. "Who?"

"My flat mates."

"You live here alone." Simon's statement was factual. There was no supposition in his voice. He hadn't deduced it, venturing around the rooms. He turned to look at Matthew. He seemed slightly more awake now. Alert. As if this idea he had about persuading Simon to flee was going to save him. "You really don't remember me do you?"

Matthew didn't take the time to look harder at Simon, he just shook his head.

Simon shook his head in chorus with him. "No. I don't suppose you do." He strolled around the table as Matthew watched him. He could see that he was still strung out. "What drugs have you taken?"

Matthew shook his head.

"Do I look like a copper? The mind altering substance, what was it?" Simon leaned over him and gently smiled.

"It was a small amount of crystal."

"Was that what you were on when you were in *Barnacles*, the bar on the seafront?"

Matthew stared at him. He wasn't sure what to say for the best. He shook his head, somewhat reluctantly.

"Just drink then? I see. Still no recognition?" He pulled away from Matthew and went over to the tools again. Simon fingered the biggest knife there. A chef's knife. The blade was around ten inches long. It was dull. The rivets that went through the handle were rusty. It hadn't been cleaned properly. He picked it up and carried it over to Matthew, making sure he could see it. He squirmed on the table crying out first in fear, and then in pain as he moved his arm.

"What are you going to do to me?"

Simon played the tip of the knife across Matthew's belly, still covered by a shirt. "I might open you up, like I need to be opened up. I want to see what's on the inside, you see." He drew a figure of eight with the knife, repeated. "Opening you up would only be for research's sake, obviously. Just to … you know, have a look. What is it you say? Have a looksy?" He grinned as Matthew began to shudder. Shock, probably. "You see, one of us …" he paused. "… one of us, inside of me, we'll call him Simon, for now. Simon wants to know what's inside you. He doesn't know that he wants to know, but he does." Simon looked at the confusion on Matthew's face. "I know this doesn't make a lot of sense to you, Matthew, but that really doesn't matter does it?" Simon raised the knife from Matthew's stomach and held it in the air. "Oh, by the way. It'll be two weeks, and four days."

"What?" Matthew breathed the question more than asked it.

Simon looked indignant. "Until you're found," he said. "May the sinless cast the first stone." Simon ripped Matthew's shirt open and brought the blade down slowly, pushing it against Matthew's skin. His skin flexed at first because of the dullness of the metal before giving in and allowing the blade to slide through into the body.

Matthew screamed out in pain, a scream different to that of a broken arm.

Simon slid the blade in, inch after inch. Matthew's blood bubbled out of the wound, up the knife, pooling in the flesh before pouring over the edge of his gut and down to the table. Simon sawed at the flesh, the knife making slow progress, tearing at the skin. Matthew was pleading for pity, but was barely understandable. Simon yanked the blade out, a spray of blood curling from the body, splashing warmly on his face.

Matthew flailed a little. He was staring at ceiling, blinking slowly.

Simon took his jacket off and threw it to one side. He fingered the wound gently, the flowing blood lubricating the gash. He slid his fingers into Matthew like he was finger fucking him.

Matthew breathed in short, taut, breaths.

Simon could feel something soft. It was flexible, but felt as if it were full of liquid. A water balloon. The stomach perhaps. To that things side was something long. Snake-like. It pulsed, doing something. Something very important no doubt. He removed his fingers from the wound and brought the knife back to the slit. He pinched Matthew's flesh and pulled the loose skin tight, making it easier to cut the hole bigger with the blunt knife. He cut across the body until Matthew had a grotesque grin painted in blood across his belly. A gaping maw.

Matthew groaned. He couldn't seem to verbalise, he just made the strangest of noises. He was shuddering, shaking, now.

Simon folded the skin back so that he could see inside Matthew. His blood pumped freely out of the wound, and Simon waved it away like he was trying to bail out a flooding boat. The water balloon was the stomach, he thought. Below it were some of the intestines—he didn't know which ones—and it still worked, pushing food or water—or something—rather pointlessly around Matthew's system.

Above it, he could make out the liver. It looked like pigs liver. He wondered for a second what it would taste like, then dismissed the idea. Matthew here had meth in his system. And God only knows what else. Simon poked the stomach lining with the tip of the knife. It was sturdier than the soft, pale, outer flesh of his gut. His flab. His pathetic human covering. He pushed harder and the stomach lining gave, the acid inside, brewing out, covering his organs.

Matthew screamed a little, and then stopped, blacking out.

Simon watched the acid meld with the blood, mixing into a diluted, harmless liquid. Simon pushed his finger into the tear in the stomach to feel the acid. It burned a little, but dissipated quickly. The human body was a feat of engineering, sure, but so … precarious. The rupture in the stomach caused the smell of Matthew's insides to spew into the room, finally reaching Simon's nose. He had mistreated his body to the point of shut down, such a sad state, and his bodily fluids complimented the mistreatment. Simon raised his arm and covered his nose. "Damn," he muttered.

He looked at Matthew. His face was pale from the blood loss. Simon dropped the knife into the wound, and drew in close to Matthew's face. His *face* actually smelt rancid. Simon examined him. He wasn't breathing anymore.

"Good," he said. Simon washed the blood from

his hands in the grimy sink, splashing water onto his face. He straightened and picked his jacket back up, swinging it around himself and slipping his arms back into it. He took one last look around the kitchen before returning to the hall and to the front door.

He let himself out, closing the door quietly behind him.

Two weeks and four days.

CHAPTER 16

Simon walked back down the slight incline away from the housing at the top of the high street and towards the supermarket.

I CAN FEEL YOU COMING BACK.

He weaved, probably looking like a drunk as he started to stagger. He reached up and held his head, his mind slowly regaining the control of his body. "No," he cried out. People immediately started to avoid him, walking around him like there was an unseen force field surrounding him, as he held his head and started to weep. "What have you done?" he cried, the strength in his legs going as they fell out from under him. He slumped onto the cobbles of the pedestrianised zone.

MAYBE YOU SHOULD USE YOUR INSIDE VOICE?

"What did you do?" Simon wailed loudly.

INSIDE VOICE. I CAN STILL HEAR YOU.

Simon pulled his knees up into his chest and buried his face in them. He had the image of Matthew being dissected roaming around his head. He had seen everything, heard everything that Little Simon had done. When *he* had been in control. "Who are you?" he whimpered. "What are you?"

ALL RIGHT, DON'T THEN.

Little Simon fell silent. Simon looked at his shoulder, half expecting to see him for the first time, sitting there, cross legged, flipping him off. Of course, he wasn't there. Of course. Simon looked around himself. People were walking around him pretending he wasn't there. He was sat in the middle of the high street. He shuffled around and pulled himself to his feet. When he closed his eyes he could see the pathetic meth-head bleeding out, his own hands covered in blood. He walked gingerly to the window outside Peacocks and spewed his guts up over the path. The bile burned as it came up. "Fucking hell," he muttered. He glanced over to the two women walking by, one of them with a push chair. She looked down her nose at him. It made him angry.

Simon wiped the puke from the edges of his mouth with the back of his arm and started back down the road. He didn't feel like going to the supermarket now. He felt tired. He didn't feel like himself. Little Simon had left him feeling like he was wearing a skin suit with his face on it, but it was only borrowed.

Violated.

He staggered as he walked, weaving like a drunk. Probably just as well, as it meant that people were avoiding him at all costs. He just needed to get home. Get his head straight.

There was no fucking way he was going into work tonight.

He got back to the bus stop and waited. He hung back from the queue, in case they could smell the blood on him. In case they could feel death standing shoulder to shoulder with them. He could only taste rotting sick in his mouth now. He knew his breath was going to stink. When the bus pulled up, he got on and waved his return ticket under the driver's nose, before heading to the top deck. There were kids sitting in the front, so he went to the back. Get away from them. Away from people.

Until he knew what to do.

What was happening.

CHAPTER 17

Simon stood in the shower, the water running over him. Once he'd gotten home he'd had a chance to look over himself, see if he was walking the high street splattered in gore, with people on every corner phoning the police.

Little Simon had done a pretty good job, to be honest. His face was clean. And his jacket. There was blood splashed on his shirt, but that was covered. So he just washed the memory off of him, his mind going round and around. *What had caused it? How had Little Simon taken over?*

Simon ran his fingers through his hair. He was going to get caught for sure now. He tipped his head back and opened his mouth letting the shower water fill it, then he spat it out into the bath. He glanced over to the toilet, and tensed his muscles pushing the piss he had back into his body. Then he thought, *fuck it*, and pissed in the bath, the dark yellow liquid pattering about his feet.

He kicked his leg out the bath and stepped onto the bathmat, picking up the towel and drying himself off.

Simon pulled his pants on, and a t-shirt and padded down to the kitchen, pulling a beer from the fridge. He paused, and after a second, pulled another two, before closing the door and heading to the living room. He crashed on the sofa and popped the cap off the first beer, taking a hard swig. "So come on then," he said quietly. "Tell me. Who the fuck are you?"

IT IS OF NO REAL IMPORTANCE.

"Well I kinda think it is." Simon picked up the TV remote and flicked it on. He scanned for a news channel. BBC. Always reliable. The newscaster was talking about live animal imports coming in through one of the ports nearby, but the ticker running at the bottom of the screen was saying that a body had been found in the sea off the coast of Birchingate. "You know, you just made me kill someone." He finished the first bottle. It was weak as piss French lager. Barely touching the sides as it went down.

YOU DID NOTHING. IT WAS ME.

"I don't think anyone else would see it that way." Simon rested the empty bottle on the carpet and cracked another. "You ain't my self-doubt though. That's for sure." Every time Simon closed his eyes, even for a second, he could see Matthew. His eviscerated body, there, in front of him. "So who are you?"

IT DOES NOT MATTER.

Simon put his feet up on the coffee table in front of him, and knocked the rest of the second beer back. He didn't speak to Little Simon again—even the thought of his name made Simon angry. He didn't think anything *to* him. He didn't want to engage with him. He just wanted silence in his own head.

The beer seemed to be helping.

After Simon had finished the third beer he got up and went back to the fridge. There was more in there, and with each beer it became easier to ignore Little Simon, even his presence, and the sight of Matthew was fading. He pulled three more out and weaved gently back to the sofa, before starting the fourth. He was angry. Drunk and angry. But the beer was slowly getting the better of him and his eyes were getting heavy.

Simon opened his eyes. He was still on the sofa. It was dark. He moved to see what time it was and it made his head throb. His mouth was dry. He rested his head back and closed his eyes. He'd missed work. Hadn't called in. He'd be in the shit for that, for sure. It was only once. He shouldn't lose his job over that. Surely.

He stayed there for a moment, waiting to see if Little Simon was going to make an appearance—say something condescending, perhaps. Even having been there for a few minutes, he made no sound. The thought that he had left was appealing, however, unlikely. He opened his eyes. The TV was off. Probably turned itself off after a few hours. He picked up the remote and turned it back on, allowing the TV to bathe the room in light. Then he took his phone out of his pocket and looked at the time. Nearly midnight. *What the fuck?* He'd been out for something like twelve or more hours. From a few beers?

Christ.

He had missed calls from Brett, too. And texts. The last one said that she was at the house and he wasn't there. He must have literally slept through her ringing the bell. Calling. Texting. *Fuck.* As the news played on the TV, Simon got up and went to the kitchen. It was too late for him to call her back now, it would have to wait until morning. He opened the fridge and leaned down, looking in. He scanned the salad. Nope. There was an own-brand pie from the supermarket on the shelf. It had been there best part of a week. He had regretted buying it before he'd got it home, and in the fridge it had stayed. *Meat and Potato.* He pulled it out and squinted at the ingredients. Lamb. Fine. He ripped open the cardboard and pulled the pie out. There was a brief moment when he considered heating it, then he discarded that idea, hunger winning over, and he took a bite from the fridge cold pastry. He chewed the pie around in his mouth, the filling feeling like a creamy pus filled mess when it was cold. The lamb wasn't overly great either. Gristly. Then the hangover got the better of him, and his stomach rebelled. The pie was still in his mouth. He'd not even tried to swallow it yet, when whatever he did have in his stomach decided that it was having none of this, and wanted out.

Simon had no choice but to turn and spit the half-chewed lamb and pus pie out into the sink, where he regurgitated half a gut of beer as well. He stood there, his elbows resting on the edge of the sink, staring at the pie and puke. There was something else in his stomach too. It was hard to make out—much as puked food always was—but he couldn't tell what. Fleshy something. He was sure he hadn't had a sausage roll from the bakery that morning, so it must have been from last night's dinner. Gross. He wiped his mouth with a tea towel, and went back into the living room, flicked the light on and turned the TV off. His head was thumping. He slowly climbed the stairs, went into the bedroom and started to strip. He threw his shirt on the floor in front of the wardrobe, and dropped his jeans, before stepping out of them.

He stared at himself in the mirror. He had his cock out. Weird. His eyes dropped to the jeans on the floor. His pants weren't in them. Why the fuck wasn't he wearing any pants? Fucking cheap arse French lager. Whatever next?

Simon flopped onto the bed and inhaled the smell of the pillow deeply. He could still smell Brett's perfume on it.

And he liked that.

CHAPTER 18

Damned infernal noise. The sound wrangled with Simon's earholes, around and around. He rolled about on the bed trying to pinpoint it. It wasn't his alarm. He looked at the red numbers flashing 12:00 as they had been for a good six months, ever since the last power cut. That was in the heavy winds last October. And the last time he'd set an alarm for just about anything was the last day on the job he had before this one. Fucking Security Guard at a discount clothes store. Security Guard was a posh title as well. Thug might have been better. He couldn't stomach the job after week, fingering chavs for petty theft. Speaking of not being able to stomach things …

Simon's gut growled with the sound of hunger— probably brought on by extreme emptiness. Then he remembered what he left in the sink last night and groaned, *and what the fuck was that noise?* He sat up and focused.

It was his phone.

He swung his legs from the bed and picked his jeans up patting down the pockets. He pulled the phone out. It was little surprise that it was Brett. It was eight thirty, and she must be calling on her way to work. He picked up the call. "I was about to text you." Brett immediately asked him where he was last night and Simon explained. He'd had a bad day, too much to drink and fallen asleep on the sofa. He missed out the bit about failing to go into work.

And the bit about hacking a man up.

But it didn't seem to pacify her. She was saying that there was a manhunt on the news. Something about a rape and murder in the town. They had an e-fit of someone they wanted to *talk to in line with their enquiries*, and it looked a bit like him. Simon had explained to her that these things happened all the time, and that she shouldn't worry, before they made gooey love bird noises down the phone at each other, and she ended the call, getting to work.

Simon stared at the phone for a minute, before he moved again. He was sitting on the bed stark bollock naked, and that scared him. Just a little. He quickly got dressed—including a pair of boxers—and went downstairs to the kitchen.

The sink stank of bile and half eaten pie. Simon picked it up in the tea towel he had discarded to the work top last night and threw the whole lot in the trash. He flicked the kettle on and then unlocked his phone. He browsed to the BBC's website and opened the local news link.

Brett was right. There had been an incident in the town last night and there was a photo fit of a suspect on their home page, and fucking hell did it look like him. Not in a *bang to rights*, sort of way. More in a passing glance at night, *oh, that looks a bit like you*, sort of way. At least, that was the way he was going to play it, if anybody asked. He stared at the phone for a second, knowing that the right thing to do was to call his boss next. He should explain—or lie—about getting drunk last night and not coming in to work. Better that, than turn up tonight and find that someone was already there to replace him.

He flicked the phone to the right and dialled the

Town and Country Office. Toni answered. Toni was possibly Jared's—Simon's boss's—girlfriend, or even sister. It was hard to tell the way they bickered and incestuous'd all over each other. Either way, Simon asked to speak to Jared, and Toni had said *sure, but he's pissed.*

"You know, Si, I had high hopes for you."

Simon sighed. He hated being called *Si*.

"*Si hopes*." Jared chortled down the phone. "When I was a young man, my boss told me this one thing, and now I'm going to tell you the same thing. He told me that *responsibility maketh the man*. And you know what? It took me years—*years*—to understand what he was yammering about. But I did. I finally got it, and I hope that you too finally get it, one day. And I think that you'll grow from this. I think that you'll appreciate what is going to go down here today, because you can learn from it. You can learn from what I'm saying. Do you understand me, son?"

Simon shook his head silently.

"I'm going to have to let you go, Si. I'm going to have to let you move on to newer pastures, because you let me down. Worse … you let *yourself* down. And I have to explain to my superiors why these problems occur, and I'll let them know that you were in contravention of our policies in the handbook. The handbook that you signed to say that you read and understood. And I will be sending on your P45 and paper—"

"Wanker." Simon cut off the call and stared at the phone as the screen reverted back to the BBC. Three murders in as many days. What was the world coming to? And now he had to go to Kings fucking House and sign on.

Fuck.

CHAPTER 19

You absolute bell-end. Simon watched the prick penning the word *dismissed* onto a form. The computers were down. Useless bell-end. The entrance to the social security side of the building was a different entrance to the one he would use as an employee. It had a hefty looking mofo on the door. Bald head. No brain cells. Simon had never been in this side before. It was weird because everyone looked at you like you were some sort of criminal. Even the other unemployed. There was no camaraderie or anything. Extremely disappointing, and most unpleasant. He'd been shuffled in through the doors and interrogated as to the reason he was here and then made to wait again. Then he had to fill out a couple of forms with one of those stupid half pens they use in Argos. Then wait again. And now he was sitting in front of this cunt—Clive, his name badge said. Clive. Stupid name.

"And the reason?" He looked up from the form dubiously.

"I fell asleep and missed my shift."

"Huh."

What the fuck did that mean? It seemed perfectly reasonable to Simon. He slumped back into the shitty office chair with a rip in the fabric that the Department of Social Security deemed reasonable for a customer. He'd had enough of today. Lost his fucking job. Probably pissed off Brett. Face on a wanted poster for one of the murders he didn't do.

Fuck.

"Okay," said Clive. He slipped the form into a manila folder and slid it into his drawer. "So, we'll look into your claim as soon as we can, and you'll hear from us in due course."

Simon raised an eyebrow. "That it?"

Clive smiled, but didn't speak.

"Fine." Simon pushed the chair back and stood.

PUNCH HIM IN HIS SMUG FUCKING SMILE.

Simon nodded at Clive and turned back into the throng of unemployed people milling about like this open plan office might have answers for them. It had none. He glanced at the security guard—baldy—and walked in the most straight line he could to the doors and out into the street. He headed towards the bus stop. "I thought you'd fucked off," he muttered under his breath, checking around to make sure that no one thought he was a looney. If this was going to continue he needed to get a blue tooth ear piece. It didn't matter if it worked or not, but then he could walk about like all the other wankers rambling to himself and when someone looked at him funny he could just point to his ear piece indignantly. They didn't need to know he was talking to Little Simon.

I WAS RESTING.

Simon looked to his shoulder. He didn't expect to see Little Simon there, but it was worth a try. "I want some answers." There were two plods walking on the other side of the road and Simon turned around, away from them, sidling up to the bus stop that he would normally take home from work. It meant that he was facing the entrance to the building that he normally entered and exited from, and that raised a slight pang of regret, which he discarded. No time for that.

Little Simon audibly sighed.

"What the fuck was that for?"

I JUST DON'T SEE THE POINT.

Simon noticed the man stood next to him looking at him funny, like. He flashed his best *I'm not a serial killer* smile at him and then busied himself looking at his feet. "Of what?" he whispered. "Why?"

BECAUSE IT'S TOO LATE FOR YOU TO STOP ME.

Simon stopped asking questions at that point. He was aware that Little Simon would know what he was thinking so he tried to stop doing that too. It sent a chill down his spine. Too late to stop him doing what? He supposed that remained to be seen. The bloke next to him was flicking through his phone now. He was probably looking for the e-fit that he recognised Simon from—just to be sure—before he ran out into traffic to flag down the two coppers that had passed a few minutes ago.

Simon turned away from him. The bus was coming. Good. He just wanted to get home. He looked at his phone and had a text from Brett. She was coming over tonight. He'd have to make sure they stayed in.

CHAPTER 20

Simon had jumped off the bus quickly and ducked straight into an alley that led through the middle of the estate. He was going to walk it until he was near his house, before coming out in the open. Normally he'd avoid the alleyways in the estate like the black plague. There was always—*always*—broken needles on the ground, meth and heroin, usually blood in at least two spots, and it was best not to meet anyone coming the other way. Normally, he would be afraid for his life, but after the last couple of days, he was more afraid of what might happen to *them*.

Luckily he met no one on the walk and only stopped on the way to drop into the Spar shop on the corner and grab a bottle of white wine for Brett, and a four pack of the strongest shit lager he could find. 9%. Nice. It was nearly as strong as the White Vineyard bottle of wine. He chose that one because it sounded fancy. The lot cost him nearly fifteen quid. They bagged it all up in one of those plain black carrier bags, the ones designed to hide the contents … to be discrete. However, these days, anyone carrying one of those could be labelled as a piss-head at a hundred yards. Right now, he couldn't care less, and just wanted to be home, in front of the TV, and waiting for Brett with a beer in one hand and Chinese takeaway menu in the other.

He still had to explain that he'd lost his job and was now on the dole, too.

He left the Spar and hurried along the street.

There were kids playing footie in the road and he could feel their gaze on him, judging him for coming home so early in the day with a carrier of booze. Fuck 'em. He had other things to fret about.

He wasn't happy until the front door was closed behind him and he was leaning against it. He was breathing hard. His heart was thumping unnecessarily. As he stood there the smell of vomit rode up his nose. He needed to fix that. Brett had a proper sense of smell. He took the bin from the kitchen into the back garden and up-ended it into the black wheelie bin. The stink was stronger once he'd turned it out.

What the fuck had he eaten?

He went back into the house and ran the hoover over the living room, and opened the window in the bedroom to let some air through. It was like a palace.

Back on the sofa, Simon kicked his feet up next to him and opened a weak beer from the fridge. No sense in getting shit faced before Brett arrived. He flicked on Bargain Hunt. Perfect.

Brett rapped on the living room window at about seven. He didn't tell her that he wasn't working that night—she would have asked why, on such short notice—and so she turned up just as he should have been getting home. He was sucking a polo so he didn't stink of beer, and he'd gone easy on it while watching TV. He *was* looking forward to a couple of cans of the 9% and a chow mein. He let her in and gave her a peck on the cheek. It didn't raise a look from her, so he was in the clear. He didn't smell of beer. Simon returned to the sofa and picked up the menu, waving it Brett's general direction, as she slung her coat over the back of the armchair.

"Raining," she said.

"Chinese?" he responded, grinning.

Brett nodded, heading the direction of the kitchen. "Wine?" she called.

"It's in the fridge. Grab us a can of 9% while you're there."

Brett returned a couple of minutes later with a glass of wine and a can. "Grab us a 9%," she mimicked. "You could use its name."

"Have you seen its name? Starts with a K. Could be pronounced a number of ways." She passed the can to him and he cracked it open, taking a swig. He pulled a face. The first swig always tasted a bit like cat piss until you got used to it.

Brett shook her head and took the menu from him. "Chinese," she said quietly.

Simon watched her from the corner of his eye. Perhaps now wasn't the best time to mention his job loss.

"I don't fancy it," she said, putting the menu on the arm of the sofa. She pulled out her phone and opened UberEats. "McDonalds?" she asked.

"Fine." Simon didn't really care. "I'll have a triple meal."

She nodded slowly as she tapped in the order.

Simon had sunk three of the 9%'s. He was laying on his back in the bed with Brett straddled across his chest. They were both naked, and she was frantically fingering herself. He reached around to stroke his cock as she wasn't giving it any attention at that second, and she slapped his hand away. "No," she said, her breath short. "You wait for me." She let out a short squeak of pleasure. Simon could smell her juices, as her legs tensed, as she got closer. This was the first time she ridden him like this and she seemed to be finding it most pleasurable. Granted, he wasn't about to complain at the view. As she orgasmed, she scrunched her shoulders forward, and squirted ejaculate through her fingers.

"Jesus Christ," Simon blurted. He'd never seen anything like it before.

"You shut your fucking mouth," she ordered, sticking her wet, gooey, fingers in his mouth like a gag. He licked hungrily at them. She reached around with her other hand and started to yank on his cock, grabbing it in some sort of death grip. Simon struggled a little, unable to speak, as even though he was pretty numb from the beer, it still hurt. Then he realised that his body was responding to it ... rapidly.

"Oh Gog," was all he could manage through her fingers.

She stopped tugging him and slid down his

body—aided by how wet she was now—and guided him into her. He came in no more than three strokes. Hard. Bucking, as she sat up and squeezed herself around him.

When he stopped, she stopped, fingers still in his mouth. Simon was bereft of breath, heaving air in around her fingers, his tongue still dancing around her digits. She rolled off of him and onto the sheets, equally worn. That was when the beer seemed to get the better of Simon and he could feel the room start to spin. "Shit," he mumbled.

"Yeah," she said. Brett had drunk the whole bottle of wine.

Simon closed his eyes for a second. He wanted the room to stop moving, but he wanted to cuddle, too. Brett got up from the bed. "Back in a minute," she said, leaving the room and going down to the bathroom.

Simon listened to her pee as he pulled his condom off and tossed it to the floor, under the edge of the bed.

Then the shower went on.

He opened his eyes and looked at his phone. It was only ten. Not a bad evening. He put the phone back on his bedside table, and reached down to his cock. It was just starting to go flaccid, but it hurt where she had grabbed it. It was an interesting experience, but painful. Something to be experimented with, surely.

He pulled the covers over himself and closed his eyes again. A numbing sensation rose from the back of his head as it dug into the pillow, and he listened to the running water, as he drifted away.

SHE REALLY IS SOMETHING. YES.

CHAPTER 21

Simon opened his eyes. It was dark. Still. He was a little surprised to find himself standing in the kitchen against the table, with Brett naked below him, her legs spread, and him balls deep in her. She was pinching her nipples and grunting like she was about to cum. Simon realised he had the last can of 9% in his hand, and could taste it on his tongue.

This *was* a turn up.

Simon was currently the driving force behind the fuck, and he wavered as he came around, almost spilling his beer. Brett opened her eyes and looked at him longingly. "Harder," she whispered in the darkness.

He started a rhythm, hoping it was the same as the one he was just doing … er, previously. *What in fuck's name?* Had he started sleepwalking? Sleep fucking? He looked at the beer in his hand and took a swig—it wasn't that Brett seemed to mind—sleep drinking?

"Yeah," she mumbled, closing her eyes again, pinching herself in other places.

Simon closed his eyes to try and maintain the motion of his drilling, after all, Brett was having a good time. Why spoil it? As he rolled his head back, he could feel a darkness slipping over his mind. It was like he was drifting off to sleep, right there, cock deep. He opened his eyes and lifted his head up, sinking some more of the beer. He could feel the burn of orgasm in the pit of his stomach, and Brett was moaning again. She seemed to really be digging it. He staved off the urge to finish. She tightened around his cock. She was cumming.

Simon closed his eyes again and concentrated on making sure he didn't finish before her.

LET ME.

Simon felt Little Simon in the back of his mind. He was sleepy, and was happy for Little Simon to take the reins for a few seconds. He had the knack of making sure that they didn't cum too quickly. He felt him take over. Simon relaxed into it, away from the action, but he could still feel his body moving. Like before. When he was at Matthew's. He was there, but he wasn't. He was out of the driving seat. Brett was huffing. She'd finished, and was being tortured by his cock, pushing against her tenderness until he was finished. He was grunting. He could hear himself, but he wasn't doing it.

"Pull out," she said.

Simon realised he wasn't wearing a condom. Shit. Little Simon grunted harder. He wasn't going to. He pushed into her harder, taking a long gulp of the beer.

"Pull out," she said again, this time with a little more urgency.

Simon snapped his eyes open and shook his head, clearing Little Simon out of the way. He yanked his cock out of her as he jizzed all up in her pubes, throbbing his load out, up, and onto her stomach. He let out some sort of animalistic noise of release, before Brett started giggling. "Christ," she said. "I didn't think you were going to do that in time."

Simon emptied the can down his gullet. *Quite.* He rested it on the table next to her. "You're amazing," he said.

I KNOW.

Simon shook his head and helped Brett off the table. The two of them went back through the house, the lights off. She went to the bathroom—again—and Simon returned to the bed. He looked at the time. Three in the morning. "What the fuck was that all about?"

WHATEVER DO YOU MEAN?

"You know what I mean," he hissed.

IT'S NOT MY FAULT IF YOU CAN'T PLEASE YOUR WOMAN WITHOUT ME.

"How fucking dare you take control of me while I'm a sleeping," he whispered. "Let alone fucking Brett. You leave her out of this in the future, right? And while we're on that, why don't you fuck off? I don't need you. I don't want you." He flopped back onto the pillow. "I don't even know what you are."

I'M YOU, SIMON. I'M JUST A BETTER YOU.

CHAPTER 2 2

Brett got up the next morning and left for work, leaving Simon in bed. She'd been happy with the night's activities, so Simon was grateful for that. At least she didn't suspect that Little Simon was there. He wanted rid of the little Hell goblin, but he knew there was nothing he could do about that right now. The little fucker always knew what he was thinking. Simon lay there for a few minutes, wondering if he was going to be able to slip back to sleep for a few hours before he had to get up for wor—oh. Right. No work. Then he thought that going back to sleep but giving Little Simon the option of getting back in wasn't such a good idea. He got up and showered, before dressing and hitting the kitchen for coffee.

"So what are you planning on doing with me next?" he asked.

Little Simon didn't reply. The little fuck was either sleeping, or sulking. He could be gone, Simon supposed, but every time he thought about that the little bastard flake re-appeared sooner or later. He started flicking through the jobs pages on his phone. There was no way that he was going to get enough benefits to pay for the house, so he needed an interview, stat. There were a lot of calls for carers. Simon frowned. A job was a job, but he didn't really see himself smiling sweetly at octogenarians and then wiping their arses. Taxi driver? Nah. No motor. Cleaner for the local supermarket? That was a possibility. He sighed and sat back in the chair, sipping his coffee. He frowned. Some noise coming from the street.

Fuck.

He slid the chair back and went out the back door. It was Thursday. Bin men. He grabbed his black wheelie bin and started to drag it out of the slot he kept it in and down the sideway. He could hear the truck clearly now. Shit. He got to the gate and they'd already passed the house. He pulled the bin out onto the path. "Excuse me?" he called down the road. They ignored him. Simon took one step forward and slipped. He managed to keep himself upright on the bin, but looked down at his slippers. He hadn't even thought to change them, and now he'd stepped in dog shit. "Fuck," he shouted. He glanced over to the bin men. Unsurprisingly they had ignored that, too. He kicked the side of the bin and achieved nothing other than hurting his foot and getting dog shit on the bin.

Simon pulled it back into the front garden and left it there.

He kicked his slipper off at the back door, flicking it with his toes into the middle of the grass. Then he looked at the sky. It was probably going to rain. Fuck it. He stormed back into the house, leaving his other, cleaner, slipper on the mat of the back door. Out in the hallway, he put his shoes on and dragged a coat over his shirt, leaving the house. He even gave a death stare to the bin men who were too far away to see, and probably would have ignored him anyway.

As he turned he came face to face with a small group of kids. There was maybe five of them ranging in height from his waist to his chest, however old that made them, and they were standing on the path, blocking it, staring at him. The youngest, in the front of the group, was holding a scabby looking old leather football. "Did you kill that woman?" he said.

"No I fucking didn't," Simon snapped back.

"You look like the bloke on TV."

Great. "No. It just looks like me."

The kid turned around to his mates. "He looks like the bloke on TV, did you see? He murdered that woman down by the pub. Messed her up pretty good. Fucked her face up, they said." The rest of the kids looked warily at Simon and backed away.

That was all he needed. Now his murderous doppelganger had been seen on TV by the local shitbag brigade. "It wasn't me," he shouted at them.

The kids scattered like some serial killer had just shouted at them in the street and *that* seemed to get the bin men's attention.

"Oi," one of them shouted from down the street.

"Fucking hell," Simon muttered. He turned and pulled his coat tighter around him, hiding in the collar, and stomping off in the direction of the alleyway.

He dropped his shoulders down a little once he was sheltered from the general fucking public in the alleyway. This wasn't going to help him get a job. He *should* go around and see his old man. Maybe he would know of something on the grapevine that he could get. But also, he looked like the local killer—of women—apparently, and that didn't bode well across the board. Simon stopped next to some overgrown blackberry bushes, took his phone out and opened up his internet-banking page. He stepped back into the bushes to leave himself hidden from casual glances. Simon checked his balance. He had enough cash in his account to last for maybe six weeks. That really only gave him two weeks to find a job and get cash flowing again. "Fuck," he said, pushing the phone back in his pocket. He'd regretted coming out now. He should have just gotten shit faced again.

Then he thought about Little Simon.

Or maybe not.

"Fuck," he said. "Fuck." And again. "*Fuck!*" he shouted. Simon raised his foot and kicked the wall on the other side of the alley. He felt his toes bend back and then they started to throb. "Aargh, *FUCK*. Mother fucker." He leaned back into the thorns of the black berry bush. They stabbed into his clothes—he could feel them poking through—but he ignored them. At least the pain was a feeling.

YOU'RE ANGRY.

"Go fuck yourself."

I'D PREFER TO FUCK WITH YOU.

CHAPTER 23

Simon clawed at the inside of his mind, trying to maintain control. Little Simon was taking it, and he felt like he was falling, drowning inside himself, his fingers slipping and sliding on his own consciousness. *No. Stop.* He tried to speak but couldn't. He couldn't stop him.

He was taking over again.

Simon strolled down the alleyway. He had a cheeky little smile on his face. He liked being in control, and it was getting easier to take it. He could take it when Weak Simon was drunk. He could take it when he was angry. There was getting less that he could do about it. He ran his fingers along the brick work as he walked. Sensations. *His* sensations, not the dumbed down, numbed down feelings, handed down like children's clothing from Weak Simon. Someone turned into the alleyway at the next crossing, walking towards him. It was a woman. She was staring at her phone like a zombie. She glanced up as she walked, catching Simon walking towards her and staring back. She looked back at the phone, but Simon could see the apprehension on her face. It changed. It was fear. Fear of who he was—and not in the *I've-seen-you-on-TV* sort of way, just *him*, his physical presence. She was scared of him being in the alley, like he might rob her or beat her. Rape her. *You can feel it, can't you?* He knew that Weak Simon could feel him. Not knowing what he was thinking, but he could feel his urges. Wants. Weak Simon would be aroused in the same way as he was by the power that he had over the woman.

She glanced up to him as they got closer, and he was still staring at her. She lowered her phone and looked up properly. Simon kept staring at her. He looked her right in the eyes, never breaking contact.

She was visibly scared. Shaking. She was *sure* that he was going to do something to her.

Just because he was there. *Imagine how she would feel if she knew who we really were.* Simon grinned at her as they passed close enough to touch. But he never made a move. He just shuddered in ecstasy when he was close enough to feel her terror. *You can feel that too, can't you?*

I know you can.

Simon continued down the alleyway. He turned out near Weak Simon's parent's house and strolled down the road. His parents didn't have as many kids living in the road as he did. There weren't many people around and Simon just went straight down the sideway, to the back door. He could see Weak Simon's old mum standing in the kitchen, wearing her old pink dressing gown. She was hovering over something in a frying pan, on the hob. Simon knocked gently on the door.

She jumped.

His mum held her chest and shook her head at him. She pulled the door open and shook her head again. "What are you trying to do?" she asked. "Are you trying to give me a heart attack?"

Simon smiled. Pathetic old woman. "Where's dad?" he asked.

"In the shed, where he always is."

Simon nodded. "Do you mind if I borrow the car?"

She frowned. "I don't suppose so. You'll fill it up with petrol though, before you bring it back."

"For course." He bent forward, lowering his face to that of his far smaller mum. He kissed her cheek. "Love you," he said quietly.

She reached over to the key hooks by the door and took the car key and passed it to him. "You be careful now, won't you?"

Simon winked at her. "You know me. Safe as houses." He rattled the keys at her and left, glancing over the back garden to the shed. He could see the silhouette of his dad in there. *I can come back for them later, can't I? They'll never see me coming, will they?* He smiled to himself, going back around the front to the car and jumping in. He started the engine. *What to do, what to do?*

Simon pulled out of the side road and onto the estate, and out.

A warm up before the main event, yes? Get you ready.

CHAPTER 24

Simon could feel Weak Simon clawing at the inside of him, trying to get out. He'd had control now for too long without unleashing anything on Weak Simon. Nothing to batter him back down inside. Nothing to keep him trapped in there.

It was dark now.

He was sitting in the car in the car park of one of the twenty four hour supermarkets.

Brett had called. She wanted to come over and have a repeat of last night, but he had put her off. He had felt Weak Simon stir when she had made it clear that she wanted *him*. She wanted *his* prowess. His fucking. Simon had enjoyed that little conversation greatly. It meant that she was ready. Now he just needed to get rid of Weak Simon. Tonight would help. He was going to push him over the edge.

A young guy came out the store. He was pushing a fuck ton of shit in a trolley. He walked it over to a people carrier. No good. He was shopping for a family. Simon's attention turned back to the door. It was always going to be a game of chance, but he had to play the odds. An old couple. No. A young couple. No. Teenager. A kid. No good. Fuck. He looked at his phone. He'd already been here an hour, expecting there to be little in the way of distractions. Why the fuck were all these people shopping at this time?

Simon banged his head back on the head rest. "Fucking hell," he muttered to himself. He could give it up and try finding someone leaving a pub? There was less chance of someone being alone, he reckoned, but this was—

Wait a minute.

A woman was coming out of the supermarket. She was carrying a couple of bags that were overstuffed, like she'd had to make sure everything she bought fitted into *just those two bags*. Simon watched, his interest piqued. She was waddling under the weight of them. He studied the bags quickly. They looked heavy with food. Then his eyes drifted up the woman. She wasn't fat, but she wasn't thin either.

Homely.

He grinned. She was wearing a warm wintery looking coat. Uggs. She had mid length hair and glasses. She wasn't dressed to impress. Two bags? Maybe no one at home to help? Simon opened the car door and got out. He crossed the car park until he was close to her. He could feel Weak Simon pleading for him not to do anything to her.

Weak Simon could get fucked.

Simon feigned interest in the parking sign, so that he was close to her, but not obvious. She was opening the boot of a small car. Fucking Ford Fiesta or something. She was fighting the bags and the boot. One of the bags spilled. Excellent. Simon scooted over and bent down. "Allow me," he said. He got down on one knee and took the chance to see what she had purchased while he gathered it up. Ready meals for one. Wine. Ice cream. Perfect. He scooped up the shopping and staying down on one knee he looked up at her, and smiled. "Oh my," he said, faking some sort of embarrassment. "I look like I'm about to make a fool of myself." He laughed, again, fake. "Would you take my hand in …" he looked at the box, "… lasagne?"

The woman laughed.

Hooked.

She took the ready meal and dumped it back in the bag which was now in the boot. "Thank you," she said, as Simon stood and loaded the other few items into the bag in the boot.

He placed the last frozen meal in the top of it. "I know the feeling," he said nodding to it. She frowned, unsure. "Living alone, and can't bothered to cook." He stuck his hand out. "I'm Simon," he said.

She shook his hand. "Daisy."

Simon looked her in the eyes. "What a pretty name, Daisy." He rolled the words around in his mouth, enjoying the squirming that he could feel Weak Simon doing. "Daisy, could I perchance entice you with a non-microwaved meal?" He laughed, "I know, I know, so charming." He looked away, hoping she would be flattered by his apparent and very fake coyness. "I—I," he stumbled over the words. "I just bought something for a stir fry. I know I'm being so forward—you must think me silly." Simon turned away.

"No," she said. "Wait."

Simon smiled, before dropping the look and turning back to her. "I would love to cook for you," he said, pushing his chest out. She blushed. Good. "I could come to your place, if you would feel safer, that way?"

"Well," she said. "I've never ..." she looked down at herself, maybe wondering what she'd done to suddenly garner such romantic attention.

"Please," he said quietly. "I'm not a bad cook." He smiled cheekily. She looked at him, then her car, and then back to him.

He had her.

CHAPTER 25

Simon followed Daisy as she drove to the far side of the town. The worse outcome for him here was that she was living with three other people in some sort of house-share bullshit, or she lived in a flat where there was no way he was going to get away with it. Either way, he could just fuck her off at the door, if that was the case. She'd get over it.

Daisy pulled to park in the driveway of a small detached house on the outskirts on the town. She was close to the cliff tops on the coast side. It looked like a nice place, and Simon was truly impressed. He wondered why she dressed so dowdy.

As he parked on the street, he noticed that all the lights were off in the house. Good. That meant no house mates, at least for now. She got out of her car and waved to him as he got out of his, beckoning him over. Simon remembered to get the bag out of the boot with the faux shopping in it. He hurried up to Daisy as she pulled her bags out of the car and the two of them walked up the driveway to the house. "I wasn't expecting guests," she said. "You'll have to forgive the mess."

They'll be plenty of mess. "Of course, no worries." Simon paused for her to go in first and politely waited for the invite to join her. Once inside, she flipped the lights on and went through the door at the back of the hallway into the kitchen. To the right there was a set of stairs, and one other doorway to the left. Simon followed her through to the kitchen. It was small, but well kept and well fitted. He placed his bag on the small two-seater breakfast table in the middle of the room.

She placed her bags on the draining board and started pulling out shitty frozen meals and piling them up before lifting them into a drawer in the freezer.

Simon pulled out a bottle of whiskey from the bag. "Drink?" he asked. Daisy turned and Simon could see the strange look on her face. "Oh, sorry," he said. "I wasn't expecting to be entertaining tonight and was going to partake in a tipple in front of a film. Seems a shame to not crack it now, aye?" She smiled, and nodded, turning to the cabinet in the corner and taking out two shot glasses. Simon twisted off the cap and poured them. He pushed one across the table to her and he held the other to his lips. They both drank at the same time.

"Can I help?" she asked.

Simon shook his head. "Just point me at the wok."

Daisy leaned forward and bent at the waist, pulling a small wok from the cupboard below the sink. Simon thought she was bending at an odd angle, and perhaps was … flirting? … with him. *Cute.* She placed it on the hob. "I'll go and change then." She smiled, still a little unsure, and then left towards the front door and heading up the stairs.

Simon pushed the door closed but didn't latch it so that he could hear her should she return. He peered into the bag and pulled out the chef's knife he'd brought in the store earlier. Supermarkets were great, weren't they? He pushed his hand into the bag and rifled around in the bottom. Painkillers. Herbal sleeping pills—he thought they were a good idea at the time, now not so much. One of those corkscrew bottle openers. Four leather belts. A tow rope. Bleach. He admired his murder kit. It seemed pretty cool. He poured himself another glass of whiskey and knocked it back in one go. *You can feel that, can't you?* He took the knife in one hand and bag in the other. Now was as good a time as any, he supposed. *Are you ready, Simon?*

Simon opened the door and walked silently to the bottom of the stairs. He could hear a shower running. Perfect. He went up the stairs to the landing. There was a closed door at the top—it was where the sound was coming from. Another to the right of the staircase, door pulled to, and one behind him, back along the landing. He stepped quietly to the nearest door and pushed it open a crack. Second bedroom, by the look of it, converted into a dressing room. Lot of fucking clothes. It was weird, at least to Simon, that a woman who dressed down so much to go out would have a whole room of fineries. Whatever. He hurried quietly along the hallway to the room at the front of the house. The master bedroom. He smiled. The room was all done out in a sickening amount of pink and white. White wardrobes. Pink laced white bedding. A fucking teddy bear in the middle of the pillows. Fucking hell. He slipped the bag under the edge of the bed, making sure it was covered by the top sheets, and lifted the mattress to place the knife there. Easy access. He stopped and looked at the dildo that was in the exact place he was going to put the knife. Dirty girl. Simon went around to the other side of the bed and put the knife under the mattress on that side instead.

He heard the shower stop.

Simon went back down the landing and stood at the top of the stairs. He leaned against the bannister. That didn't look cool. Against the wall? No. Maybe not jump her straight out of the shower. That might be a little too serial killer-y. He slipped back down the stairs to the hall and waited for Daisy to come out of the bathroom. When she came out, she went into another room quickly. It must have been the dressing room, or Simon would have heard her on the landing above his head. He returned to the kitchen and picked up the whiskey and the two shot glasses and returned up stairs. Setting the bottle and the glasses on the bannister, he tried to create an air of suaveness about him.

The thought of postponing the inevitable in favour of some evening bedroom shenanigans was appealing. Most of all because Weak Simon would hate it. Suddenly the door to the dressing room opened and Daisy stepped out. She wasn't paying Simon any attention at all and didn't see him at first, then her eyes filled with surprise, and then horror. She tried to cover herself with her arms as she stood there in black embroidered panties and a bra which was more lace than anything else, and see-through. "Don't be embarrassed," Simon whispered. He made sure to keep his eyes roving across her body hungrily, keeping them saucer-wide. "So … beautiful." She looked confused. Concerned, perhaps. She slowly dropped her hands to her plump stomach, wringing them nervously together.

"You shouldn't be up here," she breathed.

"Are you sorry I am?" Simon stepped to her, raising his hand and touching her hair as it curled away from her cheek.

She turned a shade of beetroot. "Now what?" she asked looking at the floor.

Simon stepped back and admired her. Her ample frame gave her larger breasts, and firm curves. He liked how much skin she had. He could feel himself getting hard in his jeans, and he reached down and adjusted himself, making it plenty obvious to her. "I—um—" He stumbled over his words again on purpose. He was going to fuck her, and Weak Simon was going to watch. But he wanted her to take charge. Make Weak Simon feel abused. Dirty. Take something else from him.

Daisy stepped forward, took his cock through his jeans and squeezed it gently. "Come on," she said. She gently pushed Simon out of her way and went down the landing to the bedroom. He watched her as she turned when she got there and winked at him, disappearing around the corner.

She's a go-er, you lucky dog. We're going to enjoy this ... whether you like it or not. Simon smiled to himself and picked up the whiskey and glasses following her down to the bedroom.

CHAPTER 26

Daisy roughly pulled down Simon's jeans. He'd barely had time to drop the whiskey bottle onto the dresser, and still had the glasses in his hand. His erection sprung high, pointing at the ceiling through his pants. She bit it, through his pants, making Simon yelp quietly. She grinned up at him, and he knew he was doing a sterling job. She stood. "You wanna fuck?"

Simon nodded. It occurred to him how different she was from the wallflower that he had met outside of the supermarket not an hour ago. *Good job,* he thought to himself. This was perfect. She pushed him backwards onto the bed and he dropped the two shot glasses, letting them roll from his grip. "Fuck me," he said quietly.

She straddled him and crawled up his body until she was on his chest, her weight stopping him from free movement. He could see a damp patch already appearing on her panties. *Fucking hell. This might actually be fun.*

Daisy grabbed his shirt at the collar and tore it open, releasing his flesh. She scratched him, hard. Simon grunted in pleasure, feeling Weak Simon inside, kicking at him, disgusted. Simon bared his teeth. "Harder," he said. Daisy complied. Her nails broke his skin, pin pricks of blood raising from the gouge. Simon could feel his erection tight in his pants. "Fuck me," he said again.

Daisy slapped him across the face. "You wait,"

she barked.

Simon grinned. "Yes boss."

The words raised a smile on her lips. "As it should be." She slipped off him and pulled his shoes off, then his jeans. "Up," she ordered. Simon slid himself up into the middle of the bed, while Daisy went around to the first wardrobe. She opened it up and pulled out two men's ties. She turned back to him and looked at his cock. "I don't like you to touch," she said. Simon raised his hands above his head and she came to the top of the bed, tying his wrist to the bedpost. Then she swapped sides and did the same to his other hand. "Try," she said, nodding at them.

Simon pulled his hands, but she'd done an average job. He could slip the ties if he wanted to, but be wasn't about to let this go by. Weak Simon was burning in demeaning self-hate. He was thinking about Brett. *Good*, he thought, mimicking Palpatine's voice in his head. *Let the hate flow through you.* He was sure she was going to ride him like a bronco now, and he was grinning at her, probably looking more than a little demented.

She nodded, happy with the ties on his wrist. She sat at the end of the bed and took the two glasses he'd let drop before pouring herself a whiskey. She knocked it back. Then did another. She was taking it like a pro—which was what Simon was hoping she was about to do with his erection. *Take it like a pro.* She returned to stand at the end of the bed facing him. "I like your prick," she said. "It's not as big as I wanted, but it'll do." This only increased Simon's smile. She knelt on the bed and crawled up his body until her lips were inches from his cock. He could feel her breath on it. She looked up at his eyes and continued forward, until her whole body was over it, and passed. She sat on his belly, and reached around behind her, unhooking her bra and slipping it off. Her breasts lolled free, larger without the restraint, and smooth, delicious looking. Simon licked his lips and she leaned forward, smothering him with them. Simon lapped at them, biting gently and suckling. "Yes," she said. Simon could feel her doing something. And she sounded distracted. She wasn't paying attention to his needs. Then she leaned back. She was holding a hypodermic needle in her left fist. It was dripping from the end. Simon looked at it, then, surprised, he looked at her. She raised one eyebrow. Simon glanced to the side. The top drawer of the bedside table was open. That was where it had come from. What the fuck? Before he managed to slip the ties, Daisy plunged the needle into his neck and jammed the plunger down. Simon tensed, and then relaxed. He couldn't stop himself. He was weakening quickly, and falling out of control. Unconsciousness hurtled towards him.

"Why," he said, drooling as his muscles went spastic.

CHAPTER 2 7

Simon's head hurt. It was throbbing, and he felt like all his blood was sloshing into his forehead. He tried to open his eyes, but they were gummed together. And there was this strange buzzing noise fading in and out.

He tried to speak but all that came out was garbled nonsense. His throat was dry. His lips chaffed.

And *then* he realised that he was back in control. Little Simon was gone. Simon wrestled with his eyelids trying to open them. The last thing he remembered was this woman tying him to the bed. One of his eyes popped open. He was face down, his head pushing into something soft. He turned his head a little. It felt like his whole body was restrained. "What the fuck," he mumbled as best he could. He was on the bed, head on a pillow, with the rest of the sheets covered in plastic tarp.

The buzzing stopped. "Oh." It was Daisy. "You're awake." She came up the bed next to him and stood there. He couldn't turn his head enough to see her properly, but he could see her pubes—nicely trimmed—and her hand, holding the vibrator that he remembered seeing under the bed. Simon took stock. It appeared that he was still on the bed, tied, but differently. His knees were underneath him, his arse in the air. His hands were tied, pulled apart backwards, and his head strapped down onto the pillow somehow. The only part of that which was *really* concerning was the arse in the air bit.

"What's going on?" he asked. At least his voice was returning. It was still husky, coarse on his throat, but still. It was up.

"Oh, you know. I don't like you to touch."

"That wasn't me," he said. His mind was twirling. How the fuck was he going to explain this? "Listen, I—"

She rustled his hair like he was a confused child. "It's okay, Baby. It won't hurt. At least, *this bit*, won't."

"What's that supposed to mean?"

Daisy walked around to the end of the bed and out of Simon's sight, then he heard her coming up the other side. He manoeuvred his head around to look the other way and she was standing by the bedside table that the needle had come from. *That's right*, he thought, *she drugged me.* He was elated for a split second as he remembered something. Then the truth of what he was happy about hit him, and he let out a limp, "Huh." Daisy pulled out a belt of some sort. She was fiddling with it. She was trying to slip it around the vibrator. Weirdly. She seemed to get it to the place she wanted it to be and then she wound the belt around herself like a chastity belt, the vibe sticking out proud like a horny teenage boys cock as he watched his first porn.

Then Simon started to pull on his restraints. "What are you going to do?" he asked. His voice was back now.

Yay.

"You wanted to fuck," she said. She left his line of sight again.

"That wasn't me," he said weakly. Simon listened to the strange sounds coming from behind him. Clicks. Something opening. A splooging sound. Slurping. *The fuck?* Then the buzzing started again and Simon started to squirm. He pulled on the binds that held him, but he couldn't see them. He flinched and tried to worm away as Daisy touched his bum. It was gentle at first, and then she slapped him hard on the left butt cheek. He squealed.

"That's right," she said. "Like a pig." She slapped him again—the other cheek.

"Fuck," he whimpered.

"As you wish," she replied.

Simon clenched as something was inserted up his anal passageway. It was too small to be the vibe, besides, the sound hadn't gotten any quieter, and he was sure that he would have felt something more. Then, whatever was up his arse moved. "Fucking hell," he screamed.

Daisy removed her fingers. "Just lubing you up," she said.

Simon could hear a smirk in her voice. He tried to wave his rear end around from side to side. "Please," he begged. "It wasn't me. I'm sick. I've got someone inside me."

"You're about to have someone else inside you," she said. Then she sniggered.

"No," Simon whined. "You're not listening. I've got problems."

The weight on the bed shifted as Daisy thrust her mass forwards and the strap-on slipped effortlessly into Simon's oiled arsehole. There was a throbbing at first, before the vibrations of the thing registered in his consciousness. He could feel it *inside* him. It felt like it was poking his guts. Then as the gentle— soothing?—vibrations radiated through him, it started to hurt. Greatly. As it wasn't something that he was experienced in, his body rebelled against the invader and it felt like every muscle he had clenched all at once, and then hit peak level cramping. "Aargh," he screamed out. "Take it out. Great. Out. Of. *Me*."

"Fat fucking chance," she said. She was moaning as she spoke. "Bite the pillow." She grunted in satisfaction.

"Are you getting off on this?" Simon asked, before taking her advice and biting down on the pillow, screaming into it. The pain lowered to a dull stabbing, but it was so fucking uncomfortable.

"Why do … you … think I'm … doing it?" Then she made a strange sound that if it were to be written down, would likely start with a z. Simon felt her shuddering as she reached a hard climax. He relaxed his tenseness believing it to be over, but she started pushing and rocking against him again. He could feel her fingers writhing about between them. Fucking hell, she was going for round two.

"Please, God," he begged. "I don't want this. This is … this is … rape."

"It's okay," she was shuddering again already. "You won't tell anyone." The end of the word flopped from her mouth as she slumped backwards on the bed, almost yanking the vibe from Simon, who screamed again—partially from relief, partially from the *yank*. It raised tears in his eyes.

"Why?" he whimpered. Simon could feel something running out of his arsehole, onto his legs and down onto the plastic.

"Something to do," she said. "Back in a minute. Legs are a bit wobbly." Simon felt the springs of the bed relax as she got up and then he listened as her footsteps padding on the carpet disappeared out onto the landing and then the stairs.

He started to sob. *What the hell.*

SHE'LL BE BACK IN A MINUTE.

"What's going on? Why did you let this happen?"

I DIDN'T *LET THIS HAPPEN*, PER SE, HOWEVER I WAS ALLOWING IT TO GO FORWARD. I JUST DIDN'T EXPECT IT TO GO THIS WAY. EXACTLY. Little Simon giggled.

"I need to get out of this. She's just fucking raped me." He spoke between sobs. "And she's acting really fucking creepy."

TRUE. BUT YOU *WERE* GOING TO CUT HER UP.

"I wasn't," Simon pleaded. "*You were.*"

There was a short period of silence where Little Simon was thinking. TRUE, he finally conceded. I TOO NOTICED THE PLASTIC. NOW THAT COULD BE JUST IN CASE YOU SHIT YOURSELF, WHICH YOU MAY OR MAY NOT HAVE ALREADY DONE. I DON'T KNOW. BUT THAT IS BESIDE THE POINT. SHE DID SAY THAT YOU WEREN'T GOING TO TALK ABOUT IT … THAT COULD BE BECAUSE YOU'LL BE TOO EMBARRASSED TO GO TO THE POLICE.

ARE YOU EMBARRASSED, OR HAVE YOU TURNED SISSY?

"Fuck off," replied Simon, angry. "I'm going to call the cops as soon as I'm out of this."

"No," came Daisy's voice. "No, you're not." She'd returned to the bedroom door without Simon noticing, being too engaged in conversation with Little Simon.

Simon craned his head around as far as he could to look at her. First, he could see she had taken off the strap-on, and was standing nude in the doorway. He could see she had damp, matted, pubes. He looked higher. She *did* have fabulous tits. "What are you going to do?" he asked.

"The same thing I do to all my bitches." Daisy revealed a long knife from the cover of her ample thigh.

CHAPTER 28

You've got to get me out of this. Simon hadn't taken his eyes from the knife as Daisy fingered the tip of the blade, flicking the edge against her thumb nail like she was testing it. He'd never seen a knife like it, not up close. It looked like it was out of Rambo or some shit. A fucking hunting knife, or whatever they were called. It had a big fucking blade on one side and a serrated edge on the other. "What are you going to do?" Simon asked, again.

"You're the twelfth. I think you told me your name, but I can't remember what it was, so I'm going to call you twelve. Now listen, Twelve ... basically, I'm going to fuck you up. Something I will enjoy greatly, as you will witness." She picked up the vibe from the top of the bedside table and waved it at him. "Then, when I've finished with you, I'll dispose of you. But you won't feel any of that." She crouched next to the bed so that Simon had a good view of her face. She grinned. She was clearly enjoying taunting him.

She's going to kill us. You have to do something.

YOU STILL SEEM TO BE UNDER THE IMPRESSION THAT I'M YOU. WELL, SI, I HATE TO BREAK IT TO YOU, BUT I'M NOT. I'M JUST ... TEMPORARILY RESIDENT HERE. I CAN MOVE ON, YOU KNOW.

No, no you can't. You have to help me.

WHY? GIVE ME ONE GOOD REASON.

Simon thought for a second. He didn't even pay

any attention to Daisy getting up and leaving his view, returning to the bottom of the bed. "I'll give you control."

"I already have it, love," replied Daisy from behind him.

"Not you." *You. I'll give you control whenever you want. I'll let you be me. Have me.* Silence. Little Simon was thinking about it. Hopefully.

THINKING.

Well, hurry up. Simon could feel Daisy get on the bed. "What are you going to do?" The answer came in the form of pain. It was on the back of his leg. It felt like a paper cut. A burn, then prolonged stinging. He muttered out an expletive.

"Tell me it hurts."

"It does," he replied. "Please don't." *Well?*

Another slash on the leg. Pain. Stinging.

"It's called Lingchi. It means lingering death. Or death by a thousand cuts. You might have heard of it."

Simon had, from some horror film. "Are you sick? I can help you. We can get you help."

"That's what they all say, but I think I'm just fine." Another cut.

Simon could feel the cuts weeping. They weren't deep enough to gush blood, but rather the pain was encompassing, but the blood not flowing.

ALL RIGHT THEN. STEP BACK.

Simon breathed out. He hoped that Little Simon

would take over without him having to do anything—
as he didn't know what to do, anyway. He could feel
him in there, stirring. Then he felt like he was sinking
into water. He resisted the urge to fight it. He let
himself drown in Little Simon's waking. He watched
as he lost all control over the body.

Over *The Simon.*

CHAPTER 2 9

Simon jumped as the blade sliced through his skin again. He smiled a little, with his face planted into the pillow where Weak Simon had left him. "I kinda dig it," he said.

"Well, there's plenty more where that came from," Daisy replied.

"Are you fingering yourself while you're doing it?" Simon slipped his hands around slowly. He used his fingers to work out how he was bound.

Daisy snorted. "Your tune has changed. What happened to *please don't hurt me*." She mocked his voice.

"You could at least give me a reach around." Simon listened to Daisy. Whatever she was doing now, she was doing it silently. All he could hear was her breathing. She was confused. She didn't know how to take him anymore. Suddenly he wasn't like the other eleven. He twisted his hand. She had made the mistake of tying his wrists before pulling them back tightly, and then not re-tightening the knot on his wrist. He could slip them at the right angle. He was sure of it. He slowly shifted his weight to the left, making sure not to make any sudden movement to alert her of what he was doing. His stomach muscles tightened as he felt her hand slid between his legs and grip his cock.

"You are hard," she said. She sounded surprised.

"I am. You couldn't just tug one out, could you?

One last time, as it were?"

Daisy began to stroke his cock slowly. "You *are* different," she said. "I thought you were just like the others … but this? This is new." She was getting quicker, and Simon could hear her breathing change. She was getting herself off as well. He twisted his wrist as far around as the human body would allow and pulled, gently, feeling as the tie rolled over his thumb. He didn't move his hand, giving nothing away. He just rested it there. She was still stroking his cock, and it was throbbing now. He could feel pre-cum dropping to the plastic below his body. And she was grunting in satisfaction. "It's going to be such a shame to kill you," she was saying. Her strokes became less methodical. She was exploding under her own touch.

Simon felt himself coming to the edge as well. "I'm going to cum," he said.

She let go of his cock, and let out a little wail as she came. The thought of denying him, in the face of death, some sort of twisted extreme pleasure for her. Simon summoned a grin and rolled over on the bed, free. Daisy stared at him, knuckles deep in her own cunt, flushed, and very, very, surprised. She was kneeling on the end of the bed, with the dresser behind her. Simon kicked out his foot, bouncing it off her voluptuous breasts and knocking her from the bed, backwards. She wobbled, but didn't have the hand free to steady herself, then tumbled back, crashing into the dresser. The back of her head collided with it with a sickening thud, before she slid from the bed to the carpet, on the floor between the end of the bed and the dresser. Simon quickly examined the back of his leg. The cuts were all in a row, close together. She really was going to keep going. Fucking bitch. He pulled the knot on his other wrist loose and picked up the blade, which she had discarded to finger fuck herself. Then he crawled to the end of the bed and looked down at her. Her ample tits were still rising and falling. Good. He grabbed his cock in his free hand and stroked himself back hard again. The human body was so easy to manipulate. "Tease," he muttered as he jacked spunk out over her prone body. "Fucking tramp."

Simon stood over her, watching. He liked the look of her body, but not as much as Brett. Brett was perfect. He felt Weak Simon clawing at him. *Too late, son. I'm here now.* He bent down and grappled with Daisy. She was still unconscious from the fall. There was a streak of blood on the white dresser, and a deep gash on her head, inside her hairline, but her skull seemed to be perfectly intact when he'd poked it. He groped around her, trying to pick her up from behind, his arms under hers, trying to get a handhold on her breasts. "Fuck." She was slipping around like a fucking whale. He got her up like a dead body and managed to roll her onto the bed. Simon huffed. Fucking hell. He went to the head of the bed and dragged her up the plastic to the pillow and then tied her off in some shit crucifixion pose. He checked the knots were solid to make sure she couldn't get out while he wasn't looking. Simon admired his handy work while scratching the back of his leg where she'd cut him. "Bitch," he muttered. He bent down and grabbed a handful of tit, giving it a squeeze.

Daisy didn't stir.

"I'll be back," he barked into her face, before heading out onto the landing. He walked along to the dressing room and stuck his head in, glancing around at the mountains of clothes, the mirrors, a wicker chair even, before going into the bathroom. Simon opened the cabinet above the sink and pushed tablet bottles and tubes of cream aside. He picked up a packet of plasters and discarded them to the sink. A roll of bandage, perfect. Simon wrapped his leg and used one of the plasters to secure it. He returned to the bedroom and poured himself a whiskey. Took a shot. He could feel Weak Simon writhing about in there. Trying to get a foot hold and push himself up. Out. Simon smiled to himself. He was stronger now. Free. Simon would have to try harder than that to get out now. He picked his jeans up and straightened them, putting them back on. His shirt was pretty fucked. Bending over Daisy he gave her a little slap on the cheek and then pinched her face to see if she was awake. Pretending, maybe. Then he returned to the dressing room and flipped through the clothes. She had a lot of different outfit looks. One rack had denim and leather. The next slutty evening wear— like a hooker. Then one with office attire. She was a pro. Simon shook his head and grinned inwardly. She really got him. If only the situation was different, he might have let her off. He would—eventually—need a General, and what better than a seasoned psycho serial killer?

But, alas, it wasn't to be. She was going to be the last piece of the puzzle to weaken Simon. Lay him to rest inside himself until his physical body was no longer needed, then he could have it back, for all he cared. But it would be too late by then.

By then, *she* would be carrying his seed.

Simon pulled a Cannibal Corpse tee from the biker rack, and slipped it on. It fitted well enough to get him home without looking indecent.

Then he heard a muffled call.

She was awake.

Simon left the dressing room and returned to the bedroom. Daisy was flopping about on the bed, trying desperately to free herself. There was something mesmerizing about her nakedness lolling on the plastic, so vulnerable, so … beautiful. Oh, for other circumstances. She stopped moving when he didn't say anything, when he just stared at her. She didn't scream out either. Simon guessed that she knew there was no use. People had been in this room screaming out for mercy many times and no one had heard.

"What are you going to do to me?" she asked. Once she'd stopped squirming like a child, she sounded surprisingly calm.

"Well," Simon said, sitting on the edge of the bed. "I could call the police. I mean, you did cut me."

"Go on then, do it," she said.

Too quick, thought Simon. "Although," he continued, "you can probably put all this down to some kink. BDSM play. Even the cuts on my leg. Especially the pegging, right?" Simon got up and went to the dressing room and got the chair, taking it back to the bedroom and putting it in the corner. He sat, and crossed his legs. "That's better," he said, pouring another whiskey. "This is good." He admired the brown liquid sloshing in the glass. "Supermarket own brand."

"So?" she asked. She was glowering at him like this was all an inconvenience, rather than she was feeling any fear, whatsoever. She certainly didn't seem to be embarrassed by her nakedness like she was before. Such a good actor.

Simon scratched at his eyebrow. "You see, it's like this." He placed his glass down and put his hands together in front of him. "I'm ... not human." He squinted. "But before you go all *oh no, he's a head case*, hear me out. You see, the body is. This is Simon. He's a loser. A fucking cleaner, would you believe?" Simon sat back and gave a jazz hand. "Well, *was*. I mean, you saw the news, didn't you? About that horribly violent attack? Yes. That was us. Simon doesn't remember of course, black out drunk, you see." He frowned. "Where was I? Oh yes. Anyway, he missed work that night and lost his job. I ... I'm a sort of formless chaos, if you will. Something that lies dormant, dreaming, like death does of life. Life beyond this is beyond me, though. So I need to propagate." He smiled a toothy grin. "I hope that clears up my position."

Daisy frowned at him, judging.

"Anyway, I need Simon—the real Simon—to stay locked up inside here so that I can propagate, and I've been doing it by beating down his humanity. Murder and such. It breaks down his psyche, and makes me a little stronger. You've actually been a great help, but I just need one more tiny favour."

She shook her head, doing her best to shrug. "Go on."

"I'm going to have to do unpleasant things to you. To finish the job."

CHAPTER 30

Simon stood over her, holding her knife. "Thousand cuts, eh?" He examined the knife. "Where did you get this from?"

"Amazon," Daisy replied, eyeing it. "You're wearing my shirt," she said.

"You seem … unafraid." He frowned. By this point he thought that she was probably going to be somewhere near shitting it.

"You're just trying to intimidate me. You'll leave soon enough. You'll probably leave me tied to the bed—like this—as a punishment, but fuck you. I'm enjoying it."

This angered Simon. He held the blade down near the skin of her breast, close enough to her face that she could see the slits of blood that had dried on the steel from when she had cut him. "Where do you think the best place to start is?" He didn't wait for a response, and hovering the blade an inch from her skin, he carried it down her body, from her breast, over her nipple, her stomach, pubes, legs. He finally rested the flat of the blade on the base of her foot. "How about here, and work my way up."

"You're bluffing," she said. There was now a tremor in her voice.

"Nuh-ha." Simon slid the fine blade across the centre of the sole of Daisy's foot. She yelped out, and then made an aroused grunt. "It sounds like you're into this shit." Simon smiled. "We'll see for how long."

"Do your worst."

"You really aren't taking this seriously are you?" Simon cut her again, half an inch above the last cut. Again, she seemed to dig it more than Simon wanted her to. Dissatisfied, he placed the knife down on the dresser and left the bedroom, going down to the kitchen. He rummaged through the cupboards until he found what he wanted and then he went back.

She was still squirming on the bed, trying to get free.

"You see, the way you seem to want to get free when I'm not in the room makes me think that a lot of this might just be bravado." He waved the bottle of Sarsons vinegar at her and winked. Then he took it to her foot. It had one of those reverse funnel tops to shake the contents out onto chips. Simon shook it above her foot wanking it like a shake weight. The brown acidic goodness squirted over her skin seeping over the paper-thin cuts on her foot, making her draw away from them.

"Fuck it," she screamed, wincing. "Okay, okay, seriously. What do you want?"

"You already know." Simon took the blade and cut again, above the others. Then again. The vinegar on her skin seeped into the cuts as they were made, amplifying her discomfort—a feeling that Simon already knew. He cut her again.

And again.

Her grunts of pleasure had subsided to pain, fear. She was trying to move away from him, from his touch, from the steel, but he bound her well. "This is *very* enjoyable," he said. "I get why you do it." He cut her again, across the bottom of her toes.

"Stop," she whisper. "Please. I'll do anything."

"Actually," Simon waved the knife at her. "You've already done just great." He walked around the side of the bed and randomly sliced Daisy's skin. Once on the shin. The other thigh. The stomach. Left breast. He held the blade by her cheek, the tip of the knife no more than an inch from her eyeball. She stared at it, unblinking. Her squirming stopped. Her uncontrollable shaking only visible where her breasts gently rocked. "You've done all I need." He ran the tip down her cheek without piercing the skin, onto her neck, and down to her breasts. Then he poked it in. She screamed out like he stuck her with a twelve inch blade, but it was only surprise—fear. He'd only pushed the steel in the smallest amount, so that the blood barely domed when he withdrew it.

"Such fun," he whispered. He did it again. Into the flesh of the other breast, and she called out all the same even though the pain she was experiencing was nowhere near justifiable compared to the scream. At least, that was what Simon thought. *How long do I need to do this for to shut you up for good?* He could feel Simon crying inside. He was a pathetic human being. This woman was going to do far worse things to him—*had* done far worse things that Simon was doing now. But the best was still to come. Things to shut Weak Simon up for good.

Simon went downstairs, leaving Daisy shaking, perhaps going into shock. She was cold, naked on the bed, on top of a plastic sheet, and now she was scared. She had realised what Simon was capable of. He lit the gas on the hob and opened a couple of the cupboards looking for the saucepans. He found a milk pan. Heavy bottomed. Perfect. Simon rested it on the heat and went back upstairs. He placed the hunting knife on the dresser and lifted the mattress pulling out the knife he'd hidden there earlier.

Daisy looked a little confused—a distraction for her, for a moment. "What the fuck?"

"Oh," Simon said, picking up the hunting knife as well. "I put it there earlier. You know, you were nearly very lucky. If only you'd off'd me a little quicker."

"You fucking psycho." She spat at him, but it didn't reach, instead flopping onto her own skin halfway down her body.

Simon couldn't disagree in all honesty. He held the two knives up together. "Yours is far more impressive than mine. And probably sharper. Stupid supermarkets." He dropped his knife onto the dresser. "I think I'll keep this, you know." He looked Daisy up, flecks of blood coming from the slits in her, the jabs. "Shall we get this started?"

"Cunt," she said.

Simon pouted at her. "Who's a griping baby?" His pursed lips turned to a smile. Simon took the knife and roamed over her body with it, occasionally pushing the cold of the flat of the blade onto her bare flesh just to see her shudder in fear. He crouched next to her, his face in line with the side of her body. Running his fingers down her skin, he said, "You know what human flesh tastes of?"

"Chicken?" She laughed nervously as she spoke.

"No. It's nearer a slow braised pork. Cooked in a water bath just under temperature, until it's flabby. Gelatinous." He stood and left the bedroom, going down to the kitchen. He got the now hot saucepan from the stove, and a pair of oven gloves.

He returned to the bedroom and placed the oven gloves on the dresser next to his kitchen knife, and carefully placed the pan on top of it. He looked at Daisy. "A heavy pan retains the heat, you know. I don't want to start a fire." She was watching him. His every move. He would say like a coiled snake, but she was caged. He looked from her to the pan. "Oh, don't worry. I'm not going to cook you or anything." He took the hunting knife and returned to her side. Crouching again, he slid the blade up her bare skin, scraping it along the flesh. Shaving the fine body hairs from it. With her arms up and out he could see the slight stretch marks her extra weight had put on her. Then he pushed the blade into the skin. A small sawing action to start the cut, and when he had something to hold, he pinched the flap of skin that had come away and pulled the knife down her body. He cut a slither from her, a rasher. It was like cutting the skin from a fish. It looked like raw donor meat. He held it up for her to see.

She hadn't screamed when he cut her. Perhaps the pain was overwhelming? Perhaps she had fallen into shock and was paralysed? Who knew, but when he held the slice of skin up for her to see, she started to howl. Not pain. Not panic. But impending death. It was like she finally understood.

Simon tossed the piece of skin onto her own

belly, and then cut another. Along the same stretch of skin, a little deeper. Another rasher of human flesh. And still she screamed. Simon stood and looked down on her. Her bravado was gone. Her fearless, killer demeanour was absent and she stared wide-eyed, screaming at him. He took the pan from the dresser and walked over to her. She followed him with her eyes, never stopping the scream. Simon held his fingers close to the base of the pan to make sure it was still hot. It was too hot to handle. He took the pan and pushed the base of it against Daisy's flesh, covering the wound that he had just cut. There was a sizzle, but not a long one, as the pan had lost some heat, but it should be enough to cauterize the wound. She stopped screaming. Thank fuck for that, he was thinking about gagging her just because she was so annoying.

He tried to remove the pan but the drop in temperature had caused it to stick to her skin. He pushed it back and forth, eventually taking the knife and sliding it carefully between the milk pan and her skin and levering it away from her. He glanced at her, and noted that he'd need to break now as she had passed out.

Simon looked at the burn on her side. The wound had stopped bleeding and where it had bled the heat had scorched the blood to black, hard and lumping, burned and scabbed to the skin. The smell was rancid. Where the burn surrounded the wound some of the skin had blistered and peeling away, leaving Daisy raw. "That look's nasty," he said.

Simon could feel Weak Simon inside him. His fight was waning. He was getting even weaker. Good.

Simon picked up the two rashers of flesh from her naked belly and returned to the chair in the corner. Sitting, he held one piece of Daisy meat up above his head and dropped it into his mouth, chewing gently on it. He could taste her sweat, salty, mixed in with the iron of her blood, and a light perfume in the background. Simon rolled it around in his mouth, savouring both the taste of her and the feeling of hate and disgust coming from Weak Simon. He swallowed it, and felt Weak Simon retching inside of him. He licked his lips and popped the second piece into his mouth.

It wasn't bad.

Pouring himself another glass of whiskey, Simon decided to explore. He returned to the ground floor and went into the living room. Daisy had a bookshelf of DVD's. He let his finger run along the spines reading the covers. He didn't recognise most of them. They looked like weird import films, and most of the titles weren't in English. He pulled one out. Asian, by the look of it. It had a woman on the front who looked like she was being tortured. He glanced at the ceiling and smiled. Very apt. He looked at the title. *Funny, it didn't look like it was about guinea pigs*. He placed it back on the shelf and sat on the sofa. He flipped the TV on to the last station she was watching. It running infomercials. It was one of those late night dating stations.

Weirdo.

He sipped on his whiskey and looked around the room. It was nice. His gaze rested on the films again. Apart from that lot. Simon heard a creak through the floor. It sounded like she had woken up again.

He went back upstairs and to the bedroom. She was awake. It looked like she had thrashed about a bit, and then given up. His knot tying skills could only be matched by a boy scout. He got the bag out from under the bed. She looked away from him, towards the wardrobes. She said nothing. She didn't scream.

Surely he hadn't knocked the fight out of her this quickly?

Simon pulled the bleach out of the bag and opened it. It made that clicking sound as the cap went around when he didn't depress it enough. He saw her flinch when it did it, but she didn't move. Simon poured it over the wound on her side. Daisy's head flipped around and she screamed the house down staring at him.

"That's better," he said. "I knew you were still in there. How are you feeling?"

Daisy started to cry. Her hardened veneer gone to the point of her being a frail pathetic woman.

Simon got the bottle opener from the bag. He straddled across Daisy's chest and held her head with his free hand, tightly across her forehead. She fought as best she could, but she was weak now, and he had the advantage of height and strength. He forced her eye open with his thumb and held it there, freakishly looking around, wild, as he lowered the corkscrew down over her. He enjoyed the feeling of seeing her so full of fright that she stopped moving entirely. Now paralysed with fear. He dropped the point of the tip of the corkscrew to her eye until it was almost touching it, and all she did was let out a slow whine.

Quiet. Then there was another noise. Wet. He looked over his shoulder. She was pissing. Simon returned his attention to her face, and gently, slowly, pierced her eyeball with the point. As soon as he was into it, he started turning the end of the screw, like he was turning it into the cork of a fine bottle of wine.

Disappointingly, however, it didn't grip on to anything and felt more like he was sliding it into a hard-boiled egg.

As Daisy screamed, all Simon could do was look disappointed. "Oh," he said, quietly, sure that he was going to enjoy that more than he did. He pulled the corkscrew free, tearing the eyeball and releasing a gloop of milky white liquid from inside. Daisy flailed while he sat on her, until she finally blacked out. This wasn't turning out to be the fun he had imagined, and he was sure that she was going to be hardier than this. He got off her and stamped his way back downstairs, taking the saucepan back and putting back on the gas. Maybe he'd try that again.

While he stood in the kitchen, his hands planted in fists on the draining board, his eyes wandered over the garden. It was well manicured. His gaze rested on the shed. He thought for a second and then decided to go have a look.

The back door was locked, but that was easily fixed with the keys on her fob, that she had discarded to the kitchen table earlier, and outside the shed wasn't locked. The garden was private, high hedged around the outside and no access to the street. Simon opened the door and stepped it. It was extremely well organised. This *Daisy*—if that was her real name— would have been quite the catch. He picked up a

Black and Decker mouse sander, which had a new clean sanding plate attached to it. Nice. There was circular saw too. The blade looked clean and sharp.

As he picked up the tools he could feel Weak Simon becoming feeble. He was flopping about inside him without the fortitude to keep going. He was crying out for Simon to stop, but his cries were getting quieter.

Simon took both the sander and the saw and left, kicking the shed door shut and returning to the house.

CHAPTER 31

Simon unrolled the extension lead across the bedroom. Daisy was muttering some unintelligible rubbish to herself, and he showed no interest in it. He needed to win the body, and this should do it. He plugged the sander in and ran his fingers over the rough surface. It seemed like a good grain to hurt. He towered over Daisy and ran his eyes over her face, staring at her. Without one eye, in such tormented suffering, she was still desirable.

Beautiful, even.

He flipped on the sander, Daisy not even flinching now, lost in her own world of madness. The small palm sized machine vibrated in his hand, reminding him of the things that had been up his arse in the last few hours. Simon smiled. While he was more than aware of it, at least Weak Simon had taken the brunt of that one. He squeezed the sander tightly and pushed it hard against Daisy's cheek. Her head snapped to the side from the pressure, but she didn't pull away from it. Simon removed the sander and looked at her skin. It was red, sure, but not chaffed to fuck like he was hoping. Shame. He could feel the empathy in Weak Simon, in there somewhere.

Oh, well. Better finish this off then.

Simon left Daisy's bedside and swapped the power cable of the sander for the saw in the extension. He pulled the trigger, and the machine burst into life. Immediately, Simon felt at one with the tool. The raw power in his hands was just so ...

cool. He released the trigger and watched as the blade spun to a stop.

He placed the machine in the gap between Daisy's thighs, and left it sit there for a moment. It didn't seem to register with her. Looking down at himself, he considered how messy this was likely to be. He should change, but equally, he wanted to *just do it*. Ramifications be damned. He settled on that.

Pulling the trigger, the blade spun to life and Simon drew it from the side up, between Daisy's legs. He watched as the spinning teeth consumed her womanhood, gouging into the bone beneath the skin as he moved upwards, cleaving her in two. The spinning blade flung tears of skin into the room, blood spraying. The smell of shit flooding out of her as he ruptured her colon. The spray turning to a faeces and blood mix, black and sticky. She screamed out in pain, but made no attempt to remove herself from the situation—not that she had much choice in that—probably able to feel the pain, but not knowing where it was coming from in her lost mind. He moved upwards to her belly.

As soon as the blade reached her guts, the skin split and blood spewed out into the room, flying from the blade and gushing out, onto the plastic covering of the bed. Intestines twirled. It was quite the show. Daisy still twitched, but that could have just be the motion created by the saw.

Simon moved up, hitting the stomach, the smell changing from burning iron to vinegary acid, and still he pushed up. The saw dropped in tone as the blade hit the breastplate, but the steel was true and he continued to cut through, to the heart, the lungs, the room awash with red. He cut through her neck, up into her skull, and through, further, until the saw broke out of the top of her head, digging into the headboard.

Simon released the trigger and let the blade spin to a stop before he yanked it free from the wood and placed it down on the floor. Daisy, well, Daisy one, and Daisy Two, lay on the bed, still. Quiet. Simon took a hold of Daisy one and pulled her away from the other half of her. Her guts and intestines—that which wasn't sprayed around the room, over the walls, the ceiling, the carpets, and of course, Simon— splooged out into the gap between the two halves of her, flooding onto the plastic. He nodded in appreciation.

He looked down at himself. His jeans were ruined. So was her Cannibal Corpse t-shirt. Simon licked the Daisy juice from his fingers like fried chicken grease. *Nice.* She really was *killer*. He giggled to himself.

In the silence of the room—that circular saw *was* fucking loud—Simon listened. Nothing. Weak Simon was finally quiet. Gone, perhaps, but not forgotten. Smiling to himself, Simon thought, *well, not yet, anyway.*

CHAPTER 3 2

Simon went down to the kitchen and took off his jeans and the t-shirt. He slung them in the washing machine and fished around looking for the powder. Finding it, he put it on a quick wash. He padded back to the bedroom and took the whiskey bottle and his glass and sat in the wicker chair in his pants, drinking.

Daisy made the room smell like a cross between a butchers shop and a boudoir. It sort of turned him on, but since he had slipped out of the chaotic nothing and into Simon he had found that his tastes had become somewhat unusual. The human hormones pouring through him didn't help. He could feel Weak Simon's urges latent in the back of him. They would probably all dissolve in time, but that wasn't his concern. Now that Simon wasn't going to interrupt, all he needed to do now was move on to Brett.

His gaze rolled over Daisy and his cock twitched. Simon took a shot of the spirit and poured another glass. He could hear the washing machine spinning and wondered how long it would take.

Daisy was going to be found in three days.

Simon didn't know how he knew these strange facts about the people that he touched, but he did. At least, it gave him insight about how safe he was. The last thing he needed right now was to get arrested for one of these stupid Simon quashing exercises.

Another shot. He decided to shower.

Simon closed Daisy's front door behind him quietly. Weirdly, the one thing he was becoming quickly used to in this stupid carbon based existence was that he now needed to eat. The hunger was real. He was carrying his bag—the one he'd brought with him last night—with the evidence of him being there. He took the whiskey—waste not, want not—and the bleach, everything else he'd brought with him, and he'd packed a sandwich. He needed to find something to do while he was waiting for the laundry to finish, and Daisy had some lovely looking beef already sliced in the fridge.

He had found a sourdough loaf, mayo, and cling film, so why not?

He left Daisy's and took Weak Simon's parents car—he supposed they were *technically* his parents too—back to his house on the estate.

Sitting at a set of traffic lights on the way, he sent a text to Brett. *Hey, Babe, not working tonight, wanna come over for dinner? I'll cook.* That should impress her, offering to cook.

Back at the house, he hid the tools of Daisy's demise under the sink and laid the sandwich out on the table for his lunch. Then he went and changed, putting the t-shirt away with some reverence in the wardrobe. He really did like the shirt.

Brett text back. She was coming at five. *And six, and seven. Maybe nine and ten too.* He giggled to himself. Well, he had to be sure, right? And it's not like she wasn't up for seconds last time. He sat back in the chair, and stared at the ceiling for a moment. What the fuck was he going to cook? Shit. He hadn't thought about that.

Opening the fridge, Simon used a back hand to move all the beer to the side to take stock on the food situation. There was no way Brett was going to give up the goods after being promised a home cooked meal if he didn't provide. He scanned the non-beer contents. Limp lettuce? Check. Cucumber that had no internal solidity? Check. Brown thing—possibly meat? Check. He slammed the fridge shut. This wasn't romantic. He opened the cupboard. So, noodles and limp lettuce? Fuck.

It didn't help that he'd been drinking practically all night.

Simon looked at the sandwich on the table. That was it. The only decent edible thing in the house was a cold beef sourdough sandwich that he'd stolen from a woman he'd cut in half. It didn't really say *let's do it like rhesus monkeys*, did it? At least he still had the car to go shopping.

He also had to learn to cook.

Fuck.

He looked at the time. At least he had a few hours.

CHAPTER 33

Simon stood in the supermarket overlooking the vegetables, with his phone in his hand, watching a Youtube video on how to make something called spinach and ricotta gnocchi. The video was playing loudly, and he was getting looks from other shoppers, but he didn't care. He was trying to work out if he needed to buy the ingredients, or try something else easier as he couldn't even pronounce the name of the fucking dish. His eyes lifted from the video to the stack of refrigerated pizzas in a cabinet over the other side. *No*, he thought, *do this properly.*

"Excuse me."

Simon was dragged out of the video by a young woman. He looked at her, half-heartedly, still listening to the instructions on the playing video. They were getting more complicated, meaning he just stared through her.

"Can I help you?"

Simon looked down her, realising she was wearing a uniform. He thumbed the video to stop, and the small corner of the supermarket lapsed into quiet. She was visibly happy about it. The woman was only young. Maybe eighteen? "I don't know," he replied. He looked around. Supermarket workers didn't normally volunteer help, did they?

She leaned in and whispered. "Look, my boss …" she waggled her eyes to indicate the middle-aged man standing a cowardly distance away, "… wanted me to get you to shut off the noise. It's quiet hour between nine and ten."

Simon looked around, glancing at the middle-aged man at the same time. It hadn't occurred to him that it was quiet in here. "What's quiet hour?" he asked.

"We turn off all the music and noise for autistic shoppers who don't like it."

He squinted at the ceiling. "Is that why it's so dark?"

She nodded. "So look, can I help you out with whatever it is you're doing. Otherwise I'll have my boss all over me later."

"Do you want me to kill him?"

The girl's face twisted into a look of surprised shock, and then she laughed. "No, that's fine. Just tell me what you're looking to buy, and I'll be your personal shopper." She smiled sweetly at him. "'Kay?"

Simon looked at her name tag. Shelly. "Okay, Shelly." He smiled at her. She seemed nice, and probably didn't deserve to work for the arsehole in the corner.

"So what are we doing?"

Simon pushed his phone back in his pocket. "Romantic meal for two, something light so that coitus is still possible—multiple times—but substantial enough that ... coitus is possible multiple times. And I can't cook."

"Too much information, but I get where you're

coming from. I use food to lay my boo all the time."

Boo, sweet. "So something simple, but impressive. Yeah?"

She nodded, and took Simon by the sleeve leading him away from the fresh fruit and veg. "Come on," she said. "What you need is a fancy ready meal and the ability to slyly re-plate things."

Simon let himself be led. It sounded like she knew what she was doing and that she was going to arrange for him to have the evening he required.

Perfect.

Over the next hour, Simon followed Shelly around the supermarket as she loaded things into his basket, with a running commentary on what to do with them. Mostly, it seemed to involve taking the packaging and throwing it out before Brett got there, and then putting it in the oven. It seemed a little devious and dishonest. He liked that.

He had thanked Shelly as they parted at the checkout and he asked if there was anything he could do for her as a thank you, which she had politely declined. But he had an idea. A surprise for her.

Simon loaded the bags into his trolley and wheeled it through the shop to the lift that led to the underground car park. He'd been vigilantly watching the movements of Shelly's boss as they had shopped and the weirdo creep had spent way too much time watching them. He was an older man. Maybe forty. He was thin as a rake and had a moustache. He seemed to be watching Shelly more than Simon. Then the penny had dropped and Simon realised he was one of *those* employers. He was paying extra attention to the young lady staff members.

Perv.

Paedo.

She was but a child. So when Simon had finished and was pushing his trolley across the shop he had gotten into the managers eye line and had gestured that he wanted to meet him at the lifts.

The manager had looked confused at first, but had strolled to the lifts to see what it was that Simon had wanted. He held his hands behind his back like a fucking corporal in the army. Like he was a big man, or some shit. It annoyed the fuck out of Simon, especially as Shelly probably didn't get paid enough. He quickly looked at the time, and made sure he wasn't stretching himself and increasing his to do list beyond his reach, before getting to the man and smiling at him. "You're the girl—Shelly—her employer, correct?"

The man nodded. "Correct." He was wearing a name badge. Alvin Hobbes.

"Well, Mr. Hobbes, I would like to discuss her performance. I feel that you need to take a stern hand with her." Simon pressed the button to call the lift. "But I am in such a hurry. She took up far too much of my time." The doors to the lift opened, and Simon pushed his trolley in. "Would you accompany me, while I talk to you?"

Hobbes smiled and nodded, stepping into the lift with Simon.

As the doors closed, Simon fiddled with his three carrier bags, pretending to be looking for something. "She is a bit vague, you see. And I feel that she needs a firm seeing to, if you get my meaning?" Simon glanced up to Hobbes. He could see that he had raised something in the man. His interest.

Hobbes cleared his throat. "Well, I don't really know ..." he spoke slowly, his words getting quieter, waiting for Simon to lead him somewhere. Perhaps to fuel his fantasy.

"Look." Simon straightened. "I think you might be the man for the job, but she needs someone to show her the way. Straighten her out. Do you get my meaning?"

The doors to the lift opened into the basement of the building and Simon waited until Hobbes stepped out before he pushed his trolley out behind him, letting the lift doors close. "But," Simon continued. "She also needs a man ... in other ways. Her boyfriend sounds like a total dead weight." Simon gestured towards his car, and the two men started walking. "She even said how much she respected you. How much of an influence you are."

"Really?" Hobbes sounded excited.

"Well." They got to the back of Simon's car. He opened the boot. "I'm sure there's something you can do with that information." Simon glanced around the car park. "I think she could use *your* influence."

Hobbes nodded.

Simon reached down into the first bag in the basket and wrapped his fingers around a can of Spam—something he'd picked up aside from the food that Shelly was recommending. He had no intention of using it for dinner tonight.

"Thank you for your candour." Hobbes was almost glowing. He looked disgustingly horny, too. "I must be going." He turned away to return to the lift—and presumably go and harass Shelly further, now with the intention of actually bedding her and not just fantasising about her as he whacked himself off in the shower.

Simon's hand tightened around his Spam and he cracked it with all his might on the back of Hobbes head. Hobbes dropped like a concrete block, falling into a heap next to the trolley. "You worthless piece of shit," Simon muttered. He wrinkled his nose as he looked at the can of Spam. He'd managed to hit Hobbes hard enough to split it open. He leaned down and looked at Hobbes' head. He'd also split that open—like a tomato he'd stood on. "Jesus, man, what are you made of, margarine?" Simon gathered him up and pushed him into the boot of the car, tossing the Spam on top of him. It was so much easier moving a prone body that was dressed. Closing the boot, he took his bags and put them on the back seat of the car. He was sure Hobbes wasn't dead, so he didn't want to hang around too long.

Simon ran the trolley across to the area that you were supposed to put them back, and then ran back to the car and jumped in, taking off for home.

CHAPTER 34

Simon parked the car and got out, picking up the carrier bags from the back seat and going quickly into his house. He put them down in the hall and ran into the kitchen, going to the carrier under the sink and pulling out Daisy's knife. "You beauty," he said. He could feel her blood, still sticky on the handle.

Admittedly, the circular saw was a great little tool, but it made everything within a ten-metre radius wet. Perhaps, next time, he might try a less aggressive saw.

Simon went back out to the street, holding the knife in the fold of his jacket. He checked up and down the road. There didn't seem to be anyone about, and it was the middle of a school day, so there shouldn't be any kids, but the little fuckers around here were always playing hooky.

He opened the boot of the car, and Hobbes moved. Only a little. The sudden influx of light might have jarred him back to some state of consciousness, but he must have been out before hand, because he hadn't gotten as far as banging to get out or anything. He half turned, his head matted with gloopy blood and there was a flap of skin where the Spam had opened him up. His eyes were open, but there didn't seem to be a great deal of recognition there. He was still trying to get his bearings, possibly.

Simon pulled the hunting knife from his jacket, and stabbed it into Hobbes. He was furled up pretty good in the boot, so Simon didn't really know where the blade was going, but he felt the friction of the blade sliding in. He was still impressed with the knife. Either way, Hobbes made some dull sounds of agony, and Simon withdrew the blade, sticking it in again. In and out like Joe Pesci in Goodfellas, over and over, until Hobbes had made the last of his death throes. A little out of breath, Simon glanced the street quickly, and closed the boot. He'd have to get rid of the body later, as he had to prep their dinner now, built on a bridge of fabricated culinary expertise.

And if he was going to stick around in this body for any time at all, maybe he should start doing some cardio. He slipped the knife away and returned to the house, wondering if he should put the knife in the dishwasher, or hand wash it.

Hand wash it, perhaps. He didn't want it dulled.

Simon put the knife in the sink and started to sort through the shopping. He still had hours before Brett arrived, and Shelly had done him proud with the groceries. It wasn't going to take him more than a few moments to get dinner in the oven. He thought fondly of her, thinking that perhaps once his seed had taken charge, he should see if he could arrange for her to be one of the last to die in servitude to the new chaos.

Chaos Jr., if you will.

Simon got the whiskey back out and poured himself a larger glass than he had partaken in when he was at Daisy's. He went into the living room and flicked the TV on. Homes Under the Hammer. He sat on the sofa and sipped his drink, feeling the warmth as it slipped down inside him. *What utter bollocks.* This little plump man was telling the camera that this house would do up nicely. Simon would have just steam-rollered the thing. He flipped through some channels and finished the glass.

This wouldn't do.

He was already fidgeting and Brett wouldn't be around for at least five more hours. He went upstairs to shower.

Maybe have a practice wank.

CHAPTER 35

Simon was wearing some half-decent clothing when Brett rung the front door bell. He had found this stupid apron that said, *who wants a sausage?*, on the front, and he was wearing that, too. He thought it might lighten the mood.

He'd done his best to transfer his ready meals from the plastic containers to a baking tray, he'd poured two glasses of wine, and even brushed his teeth so he didn't smell like whiskey. He opened the door and she looked him up and down quickly and then threw her arms around him like she hadn't seen him in a week. She had come straight from work and was wearing her office suit—a mid-length skirt, white blouse, and a jacket.

Honestly, though, what with the last couple of days being the way they had, it did feel like a while. They kissed tenderly at the door and then she went through to the kitchen, as he closed the door and then followed her.

"Wow," she said, taking her jacket off and draping it over the back of one of the chairs. "Smells great. I could get used to this."

Simon smiled and took the wine glass from beside his place setting, raising it in a toast. "To us," he said.

Brett raised her glass and they drank. She seemed happy with the way he was presenting tonight. But then, she was used to Weak Simon. He placed his glass back down and opened the door of the oven a crack, *checking* the state of the dinner. Of course, it was just warming through. "It'll only be a few minutes," he said. He was all smiles tonight. "You look good enough to eat," he said, coyly. Brett giggled. *Good.*

Simon served up two scallop starters onto two of the smaller plates he found in the cupboard. Then he focussed on Brett while the main stayed in the oven. He asked her about her day—and yesterday—it was all very boring, but he kept up the pretence of being interested. *Invested.* He'd spent more time with Weak Simon than she had, and although his charm offensive was on the go, he had Weak Simon's mannerisms down to such a degree that she couldn't tell that there was anything amiss.

Tedious to the max, Simon thought, but he was going for the end game. Brett finished the glass of wine, and Simon poured another for her without drawing attention to it. Then they moved on to the mains.

Simon fished a carbonara tray bake out of the oven and dished it out between two pristine white bowls. Garlic bread on the side. All premade. Packaging already in the wheelie bin outside. That was Shelly's idea—dispose of the evidence properly. She'd said something about Come Dine with Me after that but he wasn't really listening. He put the bowls on the table and topped up Brett's wine. She drank. They ate.

Chocolate torte for pudding. Shelly had assured him that he needed to buy the extra special one of those because Brett was never going to believe he'd made a pud too—which after seeing it, Simon tended to agree—and that he needed to finish a romantic meal, expecting coitus, on a high. He even had a bottle of desert wine—whatever the fuck that was—to go with it.

Between the wine, desert wine, and now the glasses of whiskey the two of them were enjoying on the sofa, Brett was acting pretty well gone. She was giggly and touchy-feely. Simon flicked on the TV. He'd left it on one of the movie channels and it was getting later now. There was a scary movie playing.

He paid it little attention, but there seemed to be scantily clad co-eds getting some party together in a soft furnishing store in a shopping mall. Which didn't make a whole heap of sense. "I don't have work in the morning," Brett said.

Good. Simon was happy to get her shit-faced before impregnating her. With him now in control, the seed was his. The child would be too. But he needed to make sure, and if that meant doing her in the morning too, then so be it. She looked at the TV screen and one of the *teens*—thirty year old actresses—was pulling off her top to reveal large, manufactured breasts. Simon followed her gaze, and wondered how many men found that tantalizing, when Brett caught his stare.

"Hey," she said. "How about you focus on me?" She rolled from sitting next to him, to straddling across his lap in one motion. There, she pulled her shirt off over her head, revealing a lacy black bra underneath. She leaned forward and kissed him. Simon enjoyed kissing her back, if for no other reason than it was a step closer to where he needed to be.

"You know I only have eyes for you," he said.

She leaned back and took his hand placing it on her breast. He squeezed, and sat up, kissing her neck. She moaned, enjoying his touch. He was being tender. She liked tender sometimes. His time in Weak Simon had taught him that. But she also liked it other ways as his time behind Weak Simon's back had allowed him to experience. If only Weak Simon had stayed unconscious that time, this might not be necessary. He slipped his hand under the lace, and squeezed her breast, pinching her nipple between his fingers. She was breathing hard, moving back and forth on him, riding him with their clothes between them. "Fucking hell," she whispered. She rocked back, off him and stood, between him and TV. Simon started to stand too, expecting her to take his hand and lead him to the bedroom, but she put her hand on his chest and pushed him back. She got down onto her knees and started to fiddle with his belt.

Oh no.

He didn't want that. He needed the seed. Simon's stupid human body only produced so much of it, and while he could manufacture an erect cock with ease— even after he had cum several times—he couldn't keep producing baby batter. "Hey," he said. "You first."

She grinned from behind his knees. "Really?"

Weak Simon must be shit at this. He slid out from under her grasp and swapped positions with her, leaving her sitting on the edge of the sofa. He reached under her skirt, pushing it gently up and she flopped back onto the sofa. She was wearing stockings, black lace panties. Slutty thin ones. Why was she wearing those to work, when he hadn't asked her over to dinner until she was already there? Who really cared? It's not like he was bothered if she was fucking someone else.

Weak Simon stirred. Down there, somewhere, the thought that Brett was getting someone else's cock to scratch the inside of her *did* seemed to bother him. Simon pushed him aside. He was still weak, even if he was awake. Simon gently pulled Brett's panties to the side. He could smell her fresh moist cunt. She wanted cock. Good. He licked her lips, gently, playfully. She moaned with some satisfaction. He kept lapping at her as she tried to close her legs on him and keep him in that position. Simon pulled back, away from her, and pushed her skirt up like it was cummerbund. Then he roughly pulled her panties down, over her stockings, passed her knees. He spread her legs like she was a whore and stuck his tongue in her snatch. Flicking it in and out like a viper.

Brett groaned. "Eat my cunt," she said. "You bitch. Eat it."

Simon worked his tongue on her clit until she was shuddering, a prolonged orgasm flooding over her, as if she hadn't felt the touch of a good tongue in forever. Simon was hard now. He gotten himself up while he was going down. He flicked his tongue over her, each touch giving her another taste of ecstasy, as he pulled his trousers down and released his cock. He straightened on his knees, and lined himself up to penetrate her, when she raised her feet, put them together in front of him and rested them on his chest.

"Easy there, big boy." She grinned at him. "You'll get yours in a minute. Get the whiskey bottle."

Damn. "As you wish." Simon got up, his proud cock swinging freely, as he returned to the kitchen and got the bottle, and two shot glasses. When he came back to the living room, Brett was gone—to the bedroom presumably—and the teens on the TV were fucking on a sofa in what looked like a shit DFS in the middle of the night. Very unrealistic. Simon realised he was going flaccid, and made himself erect again, before he got to the top of the stairs.

C H A P T E R   3 6

Simon could hear Brett in the bedroom. She sounded like she was fucking herself. Wow. If only Weak Simon had been able to get her like this, he wouldn't have known what to do with her. He walked to the door and she was laying on the bed. She was half-heartedly fingering herself and seemed pleased to see him—or at least his hard-on. Simon watched her for a few seconds and while he stood there, she touched herself while staring back at him. "Well," she finally said. "You gonna fuck me, or what?" She held her hand out for a glass, and Simon passed one over to her. She slid up onto one elbow and knocked the drink straight down. "Another," she said. Simon poured it, and again, she downed it like a sailor that had just shored.

A weaker man—or perhaps an actual man—might have been weirded out by the fact that she seemed to be downing alcohol as quickly as he could pour it. It did little for human's self-esteem, knowing that their partner needed to be wasted to fuck them, but he didn't care. As long as she took the seed.

She put her glass on the night table and used the same hand to wrap a fist around his cock. She yanked on it a couple of times, satisfied with it's apparent hardness. "In me," she said. Simon put the bottle down and pulled his shirt over his head, as Brett got up onto her knees.

"Fuck me," she said.

Simon got onto his knees behind her and guided

his cock into her. She moaned with pleasure as he pushed deep inside her, her back arching. "As you wish," he said for the second time. Simon rocked back and forth inside her, maintaining a rhythm. He wanted her to enjoy it enough that she didn't want him to stop, but he wanted his rocks off. The longer this went on the more chances there were that she wouldn't want the same ending as him.

Brett made an odd gawing sound and rested her face on the pillow, with Simon finding new depths as she did. He was getting close. He could feel her wetness. The slip and slide inside her was easy. Free. It felt good. Suddenly she lifted her head. "Are you wearing a rubber?" she asked. She spoke quietly, trying not to disturb their oneness, but with some urgency.

"I'll pull out," Simon lied.

Brett pulled forward, off his cock. "Fuck that," she said. "You were sloppy with that last time."

God fucking damn it.

She turned over and opened the drawer of the bedside table and pulled out a box of condoms, taking one out and opening it. Simon just knelt there. His mind was racing, trying to work out how to get around this. Then the thought crossed his mind just to punch her out and rape her. It wasn't ideal. She still needed to carry the child to term—not likely when it was a rape baby.

Weak Simon stirred again. He was waking. The threat to Brett. *Damn it*. This was all going wrong. While his mind was somewhere else, Brett had slipped the rubber over his cock and was back on her knees. *Right.* Simon slid into her and started to fuck her a little harder this time. She seemed to enjoy it nonetheless. He pounded on her, listening to her reach orgasm again, this time quickly. Apparently she liked it rough, then he made some faux shuddering as he pretended to cum, before pulling out.

Waste not, want not.

As Brett flopped down onto the sheets, she started to giggle, and Simon tore the rubber off, tossing it across the room. "Fuck me," he said. "You're amazing." His heart wasn't really into the small talk now. "Drink?"

Brett nodded into the pillow.

Simon poured her another, large whiskey. The bottle was more than half done, and he intended to get the rest of it down her, quickly. She took the glass from him and swallowed a large gulp. She reached over and took his rock hard cock with her free hand. "Still hungry?"

"Of course. How can I not be?" He touched her arse, sliding his hand over the smooth skin. He slid down behind her into a semi-spoon, while she nursed the whiskey. As soon as she had gotten passed the half way mark of the drink, he reached over and topped it up. There was some pitiful small talk, but the longer it went on the more slurred Brett's speech became. She finished the whiskey in a surprisingly short time and Simon lifted her up to sit. She was more of a dead weight now, riding high on the drink. Simon took her hand and led her to the landing. It was the same way he'd done it the other night, but this time she was wasted. At least he wasn't trying to keep it from Weak Simon this time.

Simon roughly held her to the wall, and pushed up against her back. He made sure she could feel his hardness against her. "I want you," he whispered into her ear. "I need you. So badly. Please … don't make me wait."

She forced herself around to face him, stroking his cock. "Like last time," she said.

He could see her eyelids were heavy. She was struggling under the weight of the whiskey. *Good.*

She led him downstairs to the table in the kitchen. Luckily he'd had the foresight to clear it off. She used a chair to step up, a little unsure on her feet, but got onto the table on her back. "Go on," she said.

Simon pushed himself into her, and she smiled. She looked at peace, as he rocked back and forth, carefully this time, not as rough. He didn't want her to rise to orgasm and stop him, and he didn't want to spoil the mood by breaking the table. It already had a little wobble after last time.

Brett closed her eyes.

Simon didn't stop. He didn't care if she was awake or not. He could already feel the heat burning into his loin.

No.

Little Simon pushed back hard, knocking Simon from his rhythm. Brett half opened her eyes, but Simon quickly regained his timing, her closing her eyes again and remaining smiling. He increased his speed. There was no way he thought that Weak Simon would be back. Not without his say so.

I SAID NO.

Simon struggled, his hips didn't want to do what he wanted them too. He looked down at Brett, trying to get to the final strokes. She was gone. Asleep or unconscious, it didn't matter. Simon pushed, other Simon pulled.

He just needed to be fully in control when he gave her his seed. That was all he needed. Then the child would be his. The child would have enough strength to take control of the world. He just needed to finish as himself.

From nowhere, thunder crashed across the sky outside.

Both Simon's fought for control of *The Simon*. His cock still in Brett, a broken back and forth motion continued as he held his head. "Fuck off. Get out of me," he screamed. "The body is mine," he argued back. "No. I just need some more time." Simon thrust forward, and then struggled back. He ended up away from Brett, still blacked out on the table. He dropped to his knees, still fighting inside his head. "I need to propagate," he said. NO. "I must continue, why can't you fucking die?" I AM THE BODY. I ALWAYS HAVE BEEN THE BODY. THE FLESH IS MINE.

Lightning forking in the night sky lit the kitchen, the shadow of The Simon cast on the wall, both hands on his head.

He rolled onto the floor, his head burning in pain as both Simon's clawed at the consciousness, Weak Simon pushing his hand into the face of Little Simon, neither having ownership, until they burned together.

The chaos and the flesh becoming one whole, the

formless bonding with the form. The lifeless death rebirthing.

As the weak and the little become the one.

CHAPTER 37

Simon awoke on the floor of the kitchen, curled like a foetus. Cold. Sore. He opened his eyes, shivering, as he looked around. How had he ended up here? The last thing he remembered ... he looked down at himself. He was naked. He rolled over onto his back and groaned. He felt weak. Getting to his knees, he pulled himself up on the edge of the table.

He didn't feel the same. Inside. His hands were shaking as he dragged himself into a chair. It was light. He squinted around the room trying to work out what time it was. He sat, getting his head straight enough to think about standing, and then he walked through into the living room, almost flopping onto the sofa. *What the fuck had he been drinking?*

He lay there for a few moments. His legs felt like they had marched to the ends of time and back again. His back was sore—although that could be from laying on the floor for however long he had been down there.

Simon rolled his tongue around in his mouth. It all felt very strange. It was like he had awoken in some different body. His, but not. It made little sense in his mind, addled.

The coldness got the better of him, and Simon went upstairs and dressed. He went and took a piss, looking at himself in the mirror after. His skin looked grey. It looked terrible. Bags hung under his eyes, and he was bloodshot. Maybe he'd been taking crack and couldn't remember? He laughed in his own face, even if it was a façade. He remembered very little about a lot, recently. He left the bathroom and went downstairs, flipping the kettle on. There were dishes piled in the sink. He'd had company. Brett? Must have been. Fuck. He must have gotten *so* wasted to not remember her being here.

Cooking dinner.

Getting up in the middle of the night and deciding to sleep on the kitchen tiles.

She must be pissed if she left without even covering him up.

He poured the boiling water over the coffee granules and added a couple of spoons of sugar, as he pulled his phone from his pocket and slid it onto the counter. No missed calls. *Shit.*

Simon took his coffee to the living room and sat in front of the TV. He flipped it on. Homes Under the Hammer. *Bollocks*, he thought. He flipped again. Bargain Hunt. *Fucking hell.* He turned the TV off, rather being in serene quietness than watching that shit.

Something didn't feel right.

He got up. He was feeling a little better. The aches in his legs and his back were gone. Maybe some fresh air would help?

Simon went to the front door and opened it, leaning against the door frame and looked out into the street. There were children playing in the road. Football. The little fucking human cattle were all wearing bright colours and laughing. *Come*, they were calling. *Come and eat me.*

Whoa.

Simon blinked. Where the fuck did that come from? He felt a little nausea in the pit of his stomach. He didn't move though. Watching the children was … exciting. Their smiling facing. Chubby features. Rife to be roasted on a spit, turned until their human crackling was crispy, moist, running in slick human fat. He could walk over there right now. Take one. He could bring it into the house, and tear it's arms and legs off until he could fit it in the big pot he had under the sink—the one his mum had bought him that he never knew what to cook in it. Yes. He could braise human flesh until it fell from the bone. He could kill. He could go in the house and get the hunting knife, bring it into the street. They were all fat little cunts. He could catch them all with ease, and butcher the fucking lot of them right there in the road. And if their parents came out to stop him? He'd fucking gut them too.

Simon blinked, and stepped back into the house. He closed the door and went to the sofa and sat.

What was happening to him?

He looked at his shaking hands. It was like they weren't *his* anymore. Like his body was voting against him. He dug in his pocket and dialled Brett. It just rang until the generic answer service picked it up. "Brett," Simon said. "It's me. Call me. Please. I—I don't feel right."

Simon got up and went upstairs. He looked between the bedroom and the shower. Nausea wanted him close to the toilet, but strange exhaustion wanted him in bed. Bed won out and he went and crawled under the covers.

Simon woke in darkness. He pushed the covers back. The nausea gone. He stretched his feet out and rolled his toes on the carpet. Still dressed from earlier he got out of bed and went to the kitchen. He got the hunting knife out of the bag under the sink and slid it into the back of his jeans. Then he went to the front door. Slipping on his jacket and shoes, he left the house.

He knew that they still had pictures of him circulating in response to the death of the woman a few nights ago. The one where he'd eaten her face. He remembered it so well now. He remembered everything. He knew what it all felt like, too.

He knew he was both Simon's now.

The Simon.

He headed to the alley. The cool night air was enough to straighten him out. He needed to find another job, quickly. He needed to make sure he could look after the side of him that used to be weak. But he needed to feed the other side of him, too. The dominant side.

He walked without seeing anyone for what felt like an hour, moving between alleyways. He passed his parent's house. The lights were out. Eventually he thought to check his phone. It was three in the morning. There was nowhere to go—nothing was open—apart from the McDonald's down on

Rochester Road, and the petrol station over by Tesco, so he just walked.

Four in the morning.

The streets were dead.

Simon had gotten all the way to the clifftops that ran around the outside of the town. He was sitting on a park bench looking out over the sea like some geriatric fucker down for the day, except it was the middle of the night and dark.

There was a young man walking the path between him and the cliff. He was weaving. Drunk, most likely. He looked like no one would miss him. Not tonight, anyway. Simon got to his feet and joined the path a few feet behind him. He caught up and walked next to him. The poor shmoe had no idea he was even there to start with.

"Gotta smoke?" Simon asked. Did he smoke? He didn't know anymore.

The guy fumbled in his pocket and pulled out a pack. With the cost of these things these days, this was most accommodating. He handed the whole pack to Simon. He took one and passed the pack back. The guy pocketed them, still doing nothing more to acknowledge Simon.

"Gotta light?" Simon wanted to push his luck. See how far he could get the guy to go. He couldn't believe it when he pushed his hand in his pocket and pulled out a lighter, handing it over, again without looking at him. Simon held the lighter, unsure whether he should light the cigarette or not. He didn't particularly want to hack his guts up in front of this dude. Blow his mystique and all that. But, the guy didn't seem to give two shits anyway. Simon pushed the lighter into his pocket and drew the blade from the back of his jeans. He waited until the two of them were between streetlights, and shoved the man from his feet. He stumbled, leg over leg like an old Benny Hill gag, before falling onto the concrete. Simon let out a *ha*, before straddling across the guy. He looked more confused than anything else, and Simon wondered if he had any idea what was going on. Simon stuck him in the shoulder. The blade slipped in with ease. *He really was super impressed with the manufacture on the knife.* He'd have to look it up on Amazon later and see if he could pick up a second one. Then the thought popped into his head that Hobbes was still in the back of his car and that he really should have sorted that out tonight. He pulled the blade out quickly. He didn't want fag-man here to start screaming, so he stuck the blade into the side of his neck.

Then his phone started ringing.

Simon stared into the wide—but not yet dead—eyes of the man beneath him. "Who the fuck can this be?" he asked. "At this fucking hour?" He pulled the phone out of his pocket, leaving the blade in fag-man. He was choking quietly, and struggling, but still somewhat more out of it than anything. Maybe he wasn't just drunk? Simon looked at his pupils. They *were* dilated, but it *was* dark. He looked at the phone. "Huh. It's the missus." He looked to fag-man. "Give me a second." He swiped the screen to answer it. "Hello?"

"Look." Brett was shouting. "I know it's late, but what the fuck? You got me shitfaced. Now you know

I don't mind that, and you fucked me while I wasn't compos mentis. Again, I don't really mind that, either." She sounded more unsure of herself the more she spoke. "And sorry to call so late. Or early. Whatever."

"It's fine," Simon interrupted. "I was just getting a snack."

"You fucking came inside me. That's what's pissed me off. You know I didn't want that. You know my feelings on abortion and shit. And then you did it anyway." She started to sob a little. "I thought you were different," she said. "What if I'm pregnant?"

Simon took a deep breath. "Honey, I know of a new opening for one of the manager positions at the supermarket in town. I'm going to apply for that today, and think I can get it. I'm going to save some cash, and you know what? If you are pregnant or not, I'm going to look after you. We'll do it together. We're a team, yeah?"

Fag-man hacked up some blood. Quite a lot of it, actually.

"What was that?" Brett asked.

"Oh nothing." Simon giggled. "Just my snack fighting back." He pulled the blade out of fag-man's neck and he wheezed a short sigh, before breathing no more. "How about we get together later, and discuss it?"

"Okay." Brett seemed calmer. Maybe she had thought that Simon was going to throw some cash in her face and tell her to *get rid of the bastard, I want nothing to do with it*. But he couldn't do that.

"Okay, then," he said. "You try and get some more sleep and I'll catch up with you later." He ended the call and pushed the phone back into his pocket. He looked at the guy beneath him swimming in his own blood. "I'm not hungry now," he mumbled, pushing himself up from the body. Simon slipped the knife into his jeans again and hauled the guy to the edge of the cliffs. He pushed him into the long grass, rather than over the edge, and hoped no one would find him for some time. Looking down at himself he'd managed to get covered in goo. Shit. He hurried off in the direction of the estate, hoping to get there before sun up.

Bad enough that he looked like the photo-fit on TV, but that and being covered in blood—even if it was only up to the knees. He shook his head and started to jog.

But *what if* Brett was pregnant? Was it going to be a weak normal baby? Would it be the chaotic spawn that Little Simon wanted? A little of both, like he was? He'd better get his CV sorted out when he got home.

There was a long road ahead of him. He was going to be a father.

Probably.

The End

About the Author

Ash is a British horror author. He resides in the south, in the Garden of England. He writes horror that is sometimes fantastical, sometimes grounded, but always deeply graphic, and black with humour.

Made in the USA
Las Vegas, NV
18 May 2022